Murder at the Festival

A READ BETWEEN THE WINES COZY MYSTERY SERIES
BOOK ONE

DANI SIMMS

TRILLIUM SAGE

Chapter One

It wasn't often that the park looked as festive as it did during the Winter Wine Festival. Avery hadn't been to the festival in many years, as most winters she'd been in the city. That year Le Blanc Cellars had the opportunity to represent themselves at the festival and Avery was proud to see her vineyard such a success.

It was a big deal, and the few friends she had in town made sure to remind her of it for the weeks leading up to the festival. Not only was it an opportunity for Le Blanc Cellars to get some decent marketing, but Cellar Vie Guest House was booked full for the week of the festival.

For Avery, it meant there was plenty to celebrate. And she was in the right place for a celebration. The first day of the festival had been a success, and the night was bound to be even busier. There was a popular band scheduled to play, and the air was filled with the aroma of all the best street food the city had to offer.

"Remember how we used to walk through this market looking for any fallen coins so we could buy snacks?"

Tiffany asked between sips. "It always was, and still is, the event of the year!"

Memories of those days came flooding back to her. It was a time when children could run freely through the festival without any concerns about security. Avery wished she could go back to those days before she knew what stress, grief, anger, or loneliness was. She remembered how carefree she felt as she would run through the fields, her head constantly bent down, searching for anything that seemed too shiny to be grass.

They would get completely hopped up on sugar, then go home and watch musicals until they eventually crashed. Everyone had fun then—Avery, Tiffany, and their parents. The memories were filled with laughter, music, and just the right amount of chaos.

Avery laughed. "I remember it all too well. I must admit, though, the festival is a lot more fun now that I'm old enough to drink the wine."

Avery was doing her best to take part in the conversation, but she was distracted by the beauty of the festival. It had come a long way since she'd last attended. She remembered it to be a couple of wine farms offering tastings and maybe the local karaoke bar would set up a temporary gig.

What Avery saw that night was vastly different. Strings with small lights wrapped through the air created a soft glow that could be seen from blocks away. Soft jazz filtered through the park, always at the same volume no matter where she walked.

The food was good, the atmosphere was refreshing, and she felt proud of something for the first time in a long time. She had put months of work into designing the Le Blanc Cellars stall. Everything about the wines, display, and wine-tasting experience had been perfected. And it seemed to be paying off.

To a certain extent, Avery had nothing to worry about. Her businesses were doing well, she had made friends, and she was healing from the death of her husband one day at a time. It was never going to be easy, but Avery had enough to keep her occupied.

She was about to say something to Tiffany when a stumbling man knocked the wine right out of her hand. Red wine spilled all over her and a nearby passerby. In fact, he had hit her hard enough that if Tiffany hadn't caught her, Avery would have fallen down too.

"She did it!" he yelled as he fell. "She's the one you're looking for!"

Avery stared at the man. He was a short, chubby man with pink cheeks and small round glasses. There was little about him that was attractive. He hit the ground with a loud thud, and a moment later, a small crowd gathered to help him up.

"What was that about?" Avery laughed as she inspected the wine stains on her shirt. "That, my dear, is the look of someone who has tasted far too much of what our vineyards have to offer," Tiffany replied.

When Avery glanced back, the man had been seated on a bench and left there to sober up. Tiffany and Avery headed to the ladies room in an attempt to clean out the wine stains that decorated Avery's shirt.

"Shall we wash it out with white wine?" Tiffany joked.

It was a good joke, good enough to have Avery laughing out loud. Her laughs echoed off the bathroom walls.

"Maybe if I just cover it with more wine, it will look like I dressed up for the occasion?" Avery suggested through giggles.

"Worth a try," Tiffany said.

"No, you can't be serious," Avery responded. She had been joking, but something in Tiffany's eyes said that she didn't think it was all that much of a joke. Tiffany led her back out onto the lawn, just behind the bathrooms.

Then Tiffany motioned for Avery to wait for her while she disappeared into the crowd, returning with two glasses of red wine.

"Now, hold still," Tiffany commanded.

Realizing that she really had nothing to lose and the blouse was already ruined, she nodded, giving Tiffany the go-ahead. Avery did her best to stand still between bouts of laughter as Tiffany threw two glasses of wine at her. The wine splashed, causing a huge mess on the ground at Avery's feet, but tipsiness had done a great job of dulling her embarrassment.

"That actually looks better!" Tiffany cheered.

"Except for the smell," Avery said as she blushed. "I smell like the bottom of a barrel."

"It's a wine festival," Tiffany whispered, linking her arm to Avery's. "Nobody will notice. Everything here smells like red wine."

"Isn't the mayor coming today?" Avery asked. "I heard some visitors saying something along those lines, and I thought I saw him earlier, but it was very brief."

Tiffany shrugged. "He usually comes on the first day of the festival, but I've been here all day and I haven't seen him yet. Maybe he'll come tomorrow."

"That's strange," Avery replied. "I was certain I had seen him. Maybe he only stayed for a bit."

"It's really great to see you having some fun," Tiffany said with a smile as she nudged Avery in the ribs. "Things have been hard on you. I'm happy you're able to let loose a little."

"Well, as of right now, I've decided to make it a habit to have fun," Avery joked, as she fixed her shirt.

It was the most fun that Avery had experienced in ages.

They were lucky enough to make it in time to get a spot on the lawn and watch the band perform. To Avery's surprise, she knew the words to every song they played and sang along loudly with the rest of the crowd.

For a brief moment, she felt like a teenager again. The atmosphere was the same, and everyone around her was having a good time too. With the lights that ran through the park, the smell of food cooking over a fire, and live music, she felt like nothing could possibly go wrong.

It had been a long time since Avery had allowed herself to let loose like that. She realized that perhaps she had been taking life far too seriously, and made a tipsy reminder to herself to enjoy life a little more. She wanted countless nights like the one she was having, and she felt determined to make it happen.

"Don't you have to clean up your stall?" Tiffany asked as they made their way to the parking lot.

The band had finished, and the crowd was leaving the park. Avery had always been amazed at how quickly a busy place can become completely empty. Soon, there would be nobody, and the lights would be turned off. The park would rest until the next morning when the second day of the festival would commence.

"Nah," Avery said, stepping carefully over the cables that led from behind the stage. "I've hired some young folk to do that for me. Best decision I've made so far," she joked.

Avery and Tiffany used each other for support to make sure they'd walk upright and neither of them would trip over anything in the dark. It was a habit they had formed after one too many bruises during their college years.

"Do you remember that time we tumbled down that hill

after the art exhibition?" Tiffany laughed. "I bruised every single one of my fingers and eight of my toes."

"I remember!" Avery cackled. "That was tough to explain to your parents too. What a weird injury!"

"I have to admit, though, I can feel the age in my bones. I'm eager to get into bed," Tiffany confessed.

"Yes, please," Avery agreed. "I'd like to go home, too. I'm sure Sprinkles is worried sick about me."

Something about the last statement made Tiffany laugh so hard that tears were rolling down her face. Avery didn't really understand what was so funny, but then again, that was normal in their friendship. Before they made it back to the edge of the park, they noticed a large crowd had formed.

"What's going on there?" Avery asked, tugging on Tiffany's arm. "Let's go see."

They wormed their way through the crowd, and Avery couldn't help but notice that many of the faces she passed were pale and concerned. That's when she saw the police tape. It was the drunkard from before.

His limp body sat exactly where he had been left when he'd been helped off the ground hours before. There were murmurs traveling fast through the crowd as police did their best to do their job, ignoring the questions of the spectators.

The man's wife was screaming on the sidelines, reaching for her dead husband through loud wails. For a brief moment, the woman tried to fight one of the police officers before collapsing to the ground and sobbing loudly into her hands.

"How terrible," Tiffany whispered.

One of the officers gently lifted her from the ground and ushered her away from the bench. That's when Avery understood precisely what was going on. She recognized the woman's behavior. She'd been there herself not too long ago.

The man was clearly dead. He had hardly moved since he had been placed there. The police tried desperately to usher the crowd away, and Avery took one last glance before respecting their request and walking away.

As she looked at the man, she realized he was tightly grasping a stone in his hand. She could just make out the word *Heron* painted on it in what looked like red lipstick. It seemed like a bizarre thing to reach for in his final moments.

But she had seen him when he fell, and she thought that she would have remembered him clutching onto something so odd.

"Do you think it's possible to drink yourself to death like that?" she asked, suddenly concerned for her own health and safety. "If so, then I need to start taking things easy."

Tiffany scoffed. "Not at a festival like this one, surely. Although, if you ask me, death by wine tasting doesn't sound like a bad way to go. Maybe he bumped his head when he fell?"

"How hard can you bump your head against a soft lawn?" Avery asked, frowning as she thought it all over.

The women walked in silence for a moment before Tiffany shrugged. "Maybe he just had a heart attack or something."

Avery thought it over for a moment, and then decided that a heart attack was her favorite explanation for it. It still didn't really make sense, given the man's behavior before he fell and the fact that a wine festival hardly seemed like the place to have a heart attack. Then again, Avery was no medical professional, and she couldn't think of anything else that made sense, either.

Everybody around them seemed to be discussing it, talking about the dead man and giving their own explanations for what had happened. By the time they reached the car, there were hundreds of theories traveling through the town gossip.

"A death at the wine festival," Tiffany said quietly. "Talk about a buzz kill."

It was a good joke, but Avery had a hard time laughing at it. Tiffany always had the worst timing when it came to humor. She didn't often tell jokes, but when she did, there was a strong chance that the timing was completely inappropriate.

The women hopped into a cab and headed home. The cab driver had already heard the news about the dead body. One of his friends who had attended the festival had phoned him to tell him about it. The gossip really was traveling fast.

Avery groaned. She knew that it meant the following day would be a tough one. She'd likely have to answer the same questions over again, considering that there wasn't often anything new to talk about. She didn't like getting involved with town gossip, but she needed to make some sales. She was running the vineyard, so she needed to make sure that anybody interested in their wines knew she was equally as interested in them. So, she didn't have a choice.

Chapter Two

The sun cast a bright golden glow over the wintry vineyard. Outside, Avery could hear the sounds of the bustling guesthouse as her guests started waking up. It was a noise that she found comforting. Coming from the city, often the vineyard felt too quiet for her.

The moment she moved, she was aware of the pounding in her head and the dryness in her throat. She swallowed hard, hoping she'd had the common sense to leave a glass of water out for herself before she went to bed. No such luck. "I guess past me doesn't care much about future me...or should I say, present me," she joked.

She moved slowly through the house as she prepared for the day. It had been a long time since she'd last been hungover, and she couldn't quite remember what she was supposed to do about it.

She drank some water, had some coffee, and then decided that her best bet was just to pretend that the hangover simply wasn't there. Although, she wasn't certain it would work.

It wasn't until she spotted the red lipstick in her makeup drawer that she remembered the events from the night before. A man had died at the festival.

As she crossed the damp lawn toward the tasting room, she wondered if, in the history of the festival, anyone had died before. It certainly would be a lot to keep the minds and mouths of the townsfolk busy for the next while.

"Good morning!" Charles' voice sang as she entered the tasting room.

"Shhhh," Avery hushed him as she pressed her fingers to her temples.

"Ah," he chuckled. "I guess you enjoyed the festivities then?"

"A little too much," she admitted. "I didn't see you there, so why do you look so tired?"

Charles poured Avery a cup of coffee and slid it across the counter toward her. She gratefully accepted it, rejoicing as the warm liquid poured down her throat, warming her belly. Charles knew exactly how she liked her coffee. In fact, most days, he made it better than she made it for herself.

"Well," he sighed. "I was getting some pretty decent sleep when I was called in to consult on a dead person. The case is a bit of a mystery."

"Oh," Avery said. "Yes, the drunk guy."

Charles looked at her with a frown on his face. It took her a moment to realize that perhaps referring to him as 'the drunk guy' seemed a little insensitive.

"He bumped the wine out of my hand right before he drunkenly stumbled onto the lawn," she explained. "Completely ruined my favorite blouse."

"How rude of him," Charles teased. "Sorry about your blouse."

"It's okay; we fixed it," Avery said, waving her hand through the air so Charles could continue with his story.

At that moment, Avery remembered how she had stood so that Tiffany could shower her in more wine as a feeble attempt to make the blouse look better. *How embarrassing.* She sunk her head into her hands and wished she could simply sleep the day away.

"Well, they needed me last night because half the police force had attended the festival and was far too unfit to deal with the scene."

Charles had been a police officer before working for Avery at the vineyard. And although she loved having him around, she had often wondered if he missed his job. But now she wondered if he missed it enough to go back to it. She didn't like the thought of that.

Avery chuckled. The mental image of a drunken police force somehow cheered her up enough to lift her head back up and give Charles her full attention.

"So, you consult for them?" she asked.

"Have been for a while," he admitted. "I realized there were some parts of the job that I missed. The best part about consulting is that I don't need to do any paperwork."

"And you don't have to quit your job here," Avery said sternly. "Honestly, I don't know what I would do without you."

Charles took a large sip of his coffee and smiled. It made sense to her now. She had been wondering why he seemed to be more cheerful the past few weeks. She also couldn't help but notice that he'd been in better shape.

"So, you had fun last night?" he asked, changing the subject.

"Yeah, it was alright," she said. "The concert was great, but...you know...a dead body making an appearance is enough to kill any good vibe."

Charles nodded in agreement.

"Who knows, though? Maybe he just had too much fun. It's not a bad way to go," Avery continued.

Charles placed his cup on the counter. "I don't think he died from having too much fun," he said.

Avery perked up. She looked at Charles and immediately knew that there was something he was keeping from her. She knew him well enough to know the sparkle in his eye meant that he had information that she didn't. "What do you mean?" she asked as excitement bubbled up in her belly.

"I mean, I have more information on the dead person than the rest of you, so I can tell you that it wasn't all the fun that killed him."

"So he didn't have a heart attack?" Avery snapped.

Charles sipped his coffee silently as he shook his head. Avery sat upright, swallowing what was left of the coffee in her cup before shuffling her chair closer.

"Give me the details," she said, clasping her hands in front of her.

"I don't know if you want to know," Charles laughed.

She knew he was teasing her. She didn't care. If he had information that was in any way interesting, she wanted it. She had a pretty boring day ahead of her, and she would take anything that could make it more interesting.

"Please, Charles," she begged. "I'll give you half a day off if you tell me."

The bargaining worked. Charles put down his cup and took a step closer to her. "Well, first, the stone seems to have everyone baffled," he said. "It doesn't appear to have any meaning, and they just about had to break his fingers to pry it from his hand."

"Okay, I mean, that's something, but I wouldn't say that's anything particularly interesting," Avery said, almost disappointed.

"That's not all," Charles continued. "They tested the

stone for fingerprints and found none. We have no idea where it is from."

Avery sighed. "Okay, so the stone is a bust and a dead-end. I get it. I'm not really sure this information is worth an entire half a day off."

"Well, there's always the suspected manner of death that might prove to be a little interesting," he teased.

"Tell me," Avery said with a bright smile.

"Well, it hasn't been confirmed yet," Charles explained. "But at the moment, it is suspected that the man has been poisoned. He had no obvious signs of a heart attack or any other natural cause of death, but a certain yellow tint in his eyes might point in the direction of poison."

The gasp that escaped Avery was so loud that it echoed through the empty tasting room. "He was murdered?" she asked. "At the festival?!"

Charles leaned back, satisfied with her shocked reaction to the information. "At the moment, it looks that way."

It was too much for Avery to immediately comprehend, and she didn't have the time to ask any more questions. A quick glance at her watch told her she needed to hurry up. It was the second day of the festival, and she needed to make sure everything was ready.

The second day of the festival had a vastly different atmosphere from the first. Whispered rumors about the dead man that had been found circulated unfiltered through the crowds. By the time it was late afternoon, Avery had heard nearly twenty different theories about how and why the man had died.

As usual, rumors had spread fast among the crowd, and the poor man seemed to be the main topic of discussion for the day. Almost everybody that came to taste the wines of Le Blanc Cellars had asked about him or claimed to have new information on the case.

One man even theorized that the poor man had been a spy that had been taken out for finding out some sensitive information. When Avery asked the man who would be worthy of spying on in such a small community, he simply claimed that he was not at liberty to divulge such information.

By the time the second day of the festival had come to a close, Avery felt like a walking zombie. Her feet were aching in her shoes, her brain was throbbing in her skull, and her eyes were burning in their sockets. But that night, she had signed up to help with the cleaning. So, it was still a while before she could go home and place her head on her pillow. She walked aimlessly, picking up empty wine cups and discarded paper napkins. Her only focus was to get it all done as quickly as possible so she could go home.

She found herself standing in front of the bench where the dead man had been sitting the night before. She wondered what his last moments might have been like. Knowing that he was potentially murdered, she contemplated all the reasons why somebody might have wanted him dead.

She remembered his distraught wife as she cried over her husband. Avery knew the pain the woman must have felt at that moment and felt pity for her. As she stared at the bench, she pictured the woman at home without her husband, knowing he'd never be coming back.

Avery knew well enough what it meant to lose a husband. Her husband, James, had also died, and she had reacted the way the woman at the festival had. Disbelief had poisoned her mind, and she had refused to believe that he could truly be gone. And as soon as she accepted it to be true, grief made its presence and nested itself so deep in her heart that she felt it might never beat the same again.

The memories of Avery's own pain came flooding back too quickly for her to bear. So she turned away from the bench and carried on with the task at hand. She looked for other things to focus on, hoping that all thoughts of the dead man would soon leave her and she could carry on in peace.

She was paying little attention when a small stone caught her eye. It didn't seem out of place, only that she could spot a small red mark on the back of it. Carefully, Avery lifted the stone up and turned it around. The word *The* was written on the stone in the same red that had been spotted on the stone in the dead man's hand. Avery's heart sank. She took a step back and felt a large bump beneath her feet. When she looked down to see what it was, she found another stone. On that stone was written the word *Follow*. She picked it up and held the stones side-by-side. Her heart was pounding as she stared at them, wishing it was only a dream.

"Follow the heron," she whispered.

It wasn't until she looked up from the stones that the situation became even more terrifying. They were lying right beneath the bench that the dead man had been found on. It looked as if they had simply fallen there.

"This can't be good," she whispered as she swallowed hard.

Chapter Three

Avery had abandoned all attempts at carrying on with the clean-up of the festival grounds. Instead, with the stones placed neatly on her passenger seat, she raced toward the police station.

"Follow the heron," she said. "What does it mean?!"

As it would be, she was stuck at the world's slowest traffic light, and her thoughts raced ahead of her. *What if that visitor at the stall had been right all along? What if the dead man really had been a spy? Were the stones a message to him or the police?*

She had been so deep in thought that she hadn't realized the traffic light had turned green until an impatient driver in the car behind her honked their horn.

By the time she finally made it to the station, she was breaking out in a sweat. She'd imagined that now that she'd found the stones, she would be in danger, and perhaps that car behind her was following her, and she'd be the next one found dead on the festival grounds.

She slammed the stones down on the counter, causing the police officers on duty to jump.

"Ah, Avery," said the officer. "What brings you here this evening?"

"I-I was doing the clean-up thing at the festival, and I found these two stones," she said, out of breath.

The officer reached for the stones and lifted them up. The moment the red writing was visible, every officer in the room stood up and took a few steps closer. They looked at the stones and then at each other. Then they looked back at Avery. They continued through that cycle a few more times before one of them finally spoke.

"Where did you find these exactly?" he asked.

"They were just lying there," she explained. "I found them by accident while I was cleaning up."

"Yes, I gathered," he said sarcastically. "I mean, where did you find them exactly? Was it near the bench where the man was?"

"Yes," Avery answered. "I found them directly beneath the bench that he was on. How did you not see it when you were there?"

"Forgive us, Avery," he said even more sarcastically. "But when we're dealing with a random death that hasn't been ruled a murder yet, we're not exactly looking for stones. Are we?"

There was silence as the police officer wrote the information down. Then, he pulled out some paper, drew a vague map of the park, and asked Avery to circle exactly where she had found them.

She did so, and the officer showed the rest of them and then put the paper on the counter. Avery immediately felt as if they weren't taking it seriously enough. Nobody was scrambling to make any phone calls or asking for a formal statement. It was nothing like she'd read in her husband's books or watched in a crime series.

"I saw the stone that he had in his hand yesterday. With

all three of them, it reads Follow The Heron," she explained. "I figured it would be important to the investigation since they look kinda the same."

The police officer smiled. "Yes, thank you," he said before handing the stones to another officer to tag as evidence. "You did the right thing."

"What do you think it means?" Avery asked, tears welling up in her eyes. "Do you think it has something to do with who murdered him?"

"Who said anything about murder?" the police officer asked with a frown.

Avery rolled her eyes. Every time she had ever dealt with the police, they had been nothing but completely unhelpful. Still, they were the only choice she had. "You literally just mentioned it earlier," she said with a straight face.

"Yes, you did," the officer's colleague chirped from the background.

"Oh," he replied sheepishly. "I see."

Avery had to be careful how much she said. She didn't want to get Charles into any trouble. She had seen how his face had lit up when he spoke about consulting for the police again. She didn't want to do anything to jeopardize that by blurting out information she wasn't supposed to have. She knew she couldn't mention anything about the poisoning. She wasn't supposed to know about that.

"Look," the officer sighed. "Thank you for bringing these in; we've put them in as evidence, and I'm sure we'll look into it."

"You're sure?" Avery asked, her voice wavering slightly from the stress. "You don't seem all that convinced."

"Where you found these stones doesn't make any sense," the officer explained. "At the moment, the likely scenario would be that he simply found the stone and was coincidentally holding it at the time that he was...um...he died."

"What do you mean they don't make sense?" she blurted out. "He had one in his hand, and these were right below where he was seated."

"You have to let us do our jobs," the officer said, unamused. "We're the ones with the training."

Avery knew that it was the end of the conversation. She could tell by the way the officer kept glancing toward the door that he didn't want to answer any more of her questions.

"Thank you for bringing these in, Avery. We'll be sure to look into it," he said. "Just one thing before you go. Please don't get involved in any of this. I've read your husband's books. They're fiction. It's good you brought these to us, but it's up to us now to follow it all up."

Avery sighed and left the station. On the one hand, she understood that perhaps the dead man really had just found the stone and that none of it meant anything. On the other hand, she knew there was something odd about a man potentially being poisoned at the wine festival. None of it made any sense to her, and she didn't entirely like the way the police were handling it. But she was no professional detective, and her hands were tied.

Still, as she drove home, the words *Follow The Heron* replayed over and over in her mind. The words seemed so carefully chosen. They made no sense when put in any other order, and they formed a complete sentence. They were purposefully spelling something out. It seemed like an odd thing to leave lying around.

It didn't seem like the kind of phrase a child would use, either. She replayed the conversation with the police in her mind, too. She couldn't quite decide whether or not they were taking it seriously enough, according to Avery. Then again, how much could they really do?

She felt her eyes start to burn as she considered the grieving wife. She remembered how cold the empty space in her bed had felt when her husband, James, had died. She knew the dead man's wife was going through the same thing.

Avery understood that perhaps she was taking it all too personally out of empathy for the grieving woman. When she thought about it, she could still feel how the tears had burned her cheeks after countless days of crying. It was a dull headache that lingered for weeks, and she knew that the woman she'd seen sobbing on the ground was going to go through all of it. She wondered if they had let the woman know that her husband had potentially been murdered.

By the time Avery got home, she was completely fed up with her own thoughts. Still, she couldn't help but feel that the police should be doing more.

Maybe Charles can help. She looked at the time. It was very late. But she needed to clear her head, and he was the only person who could help her do it. So, she reached for the phone and dialed his number.

"Avery, do you know what time it is?" his sleepy voice answered.

"Yes, Charles, I'm sorry," she said. "Do you have a minute to talk?"

On the other end of the line, she heard the familiar sound of ruffling blankets and the sound of a light switch.

"What's up?" he asked. "Everything okay?"

"Yes, well, kinda...I don't know," she answered. "I was doing the clean-up at the festival grounds tonight when I found two stones with red words on them."

"Like the one the man was holding?" he asked, his voice suddenly sounding much more awake.

"Exactly like those," she answered. "The one read *Follow,* and the other read *The.*"

There was a moment of silence before Charles answered. "Follow The Heron?"

"Precisely!" Avery was almost excited when she heard Charles say it. "I took them to the police to hand them in for evidence."

"You don't sound too happy about it," he said.

"Well, I am because I know it was the right thing to do," she said. "And they said they would do what they can."

"But?" Charles asked, anticipating Avery's complaint.

"But," she sighed. "They seem to think that maybe it means nothing at all and it is just coincidence then that he was holding the stone. I was hoping you could nudge them to look into it a little more."

The silence on the other end of the call carried on for a short while. Avery wished she could hurry Charles up. She was sleepy and just needed him to help her so she could relax enough to get into bed. But she also knew that she had woken him up at a ridiculous hour, so she gave him time to formulate his response.

"Where did you find the stones?" he asked.

"At the edge of the park," she answered, realizing that he was asking all the same questions as the first officer.

"You know, Avery, I'd love to help you here, but I'd have to agree with the police," he said. "It is probably just a coincidence."

Avery sighed. "Do you really think so?"

"Well, the words don't mean anything. It has nothing to do with anything at all. It could just be parts of a children's game, and he might have found that stone just the same way that you found the other two."

"Do you know if they have tested for poisoning yet?" she asked.

"Yes," he answered. "Our suspicions were right. The coroner confirmed this morning that he died of poisoning. We're waiting to hear back about exactly what kind of poison."

"So then someone was after him, and the stones could mean something?" Avery pressed.

"If this were a James Bond movie, perhaps. But this is a small-town wine festival. It could have still been an accident."

"So you agree with the police?" she asked bluntly.

"Yes, I agree with them. Now get some rest; it's very late."

"But if it is a murder like we know now," Avery continued, "then surely you have to think the stones are a message of some kind and that they hold some kind of meaning?"

"What exactly do you think they could mean?" he asked, annoyed by her persistence.

Avery thought about it for a while. "I don't know," she answered sheepishly.

"Precisely. It doesn't make sense," Charles snapped. "Now get some rest. I'm going back to bed."

Avery ended the call feeling even more frustrated than she had before. The one person she relied on to take her side was Charles, and he had done nothing to help her. She wasn't really sure why she felt so frustrated about it, either. She knew that they were right.

It did seem kind of odd and as if it meant nothing. But she knew what the dead man's wife was going through, and she knew the grieving woman would want the police to take it a little more seriously.

Chapter Four

Avery awoke after a restless night to discover that the sky was gray and overcast—much like her mood. She had spent many hours of the night imagining all the things she could have said to Charles that would either have changed his mind or made him at least as frustrated as she was.

Sprinkles snuggled up to her feet, convincing her to spend just a few more minutes in bed, and she obliged, of course. Besides, Charles was due to stop by and collect some more wine before dropping it off at their stall at the festival, and Avery was in no mood to see him.

Her bed was nice and warm, and Sprinkles did a decent job of keeping her company when she went to sleep. Still, as she stared at the empty space beside her, she couldn't help but feel pity for the dead man's wife.

She remembered the first few mornings after James died and how strange it felt not to hear his soft breathing or cheerful greetings if she'd slept in late. She wondered if the grieving woman she'd seen that night at the festival was feeling the same way. *Of course, she is.*

Avery dragged her feet through the house to start her morning routine. Feed Sprinkles, have some coffee, eat breakfast, and have another cup of coffee. Then, she would probably stare out the window for a few minutes before speeding through a shower to get ready. There wasn't enough coffee in the world that day that could fix her mood, but at the very least, she was caffeinated and had a full belly. Eggs and smoked salmon always hit the spot just right.

Avery needed to work one more day at the festival, and then Charles would take over the stall. She very much looked forward to finishing her responsibilities there. She could feel the tiredness seeping into the center of her bones, and all she wanted was a day off to sit and do nothing.

A pile of books had been taunting her for weeks. She'd been threatening to read them, but all of her time had gone to prepare for the festivities, and now the large pile of books just seemed like a tedious task on her to-do list.

Normally, her morning routine included a stop at the wine room to greet Charles and make sure he was prepared for the day. But not once had he actually needed anything from her, and she was certain if she went to see him, she wouldn't be able to bite her tongue.

She had been so certain when she phoned him the night before that he'd take her side and see things from her perspective. But he didn't and it irked her. She also couldn't shake the thought that she had annoyed him somehow.

Then, the thought of him finding her annoying only made her even more upset. The combination of all her twisted emotions toward the entire situation made her feel confused and further frustrated and only worsened her mood.

As Avery watched through the window, the gray clouds kept rolling in, and the sky only got darker. She wondered if it would mean a quieter day at the festival. If it rained, then the day might be a complete bust, and she wasn't sure she could handle something like that. They had been doing so well; she was eager to keep that ball rolling.

She thought about all the feet that had walked through the park recently and how many of them could have spotted the stones she had found. If they were left there by somebody else, then somebody would know something about it. Surely it wouldn't be too hard for the police to simply ask for more information on the stones? Of course, they wouldn't, as they'd already decided that the stones were simply a coincidence.

Frustrated and eager to let it go, Avery decided to shower and prepare for the day. As she washed her hair, she tried desperately to rinse away all thoughts of the murder and the stones. She had other things to focus on. But it was no use. By the time she stepped out of the shower, she had already envisioned multiple false scenarios and conversations, and she was only more irritated with Charles and frustrated with the entire situation at hand.

"That's it," she mumbled. "I'm just going to have to prove him wrong."

With a determined stride, she marched over to her laptop. It took her a few minutes to choose the right font and font size, but by the time she was done printing the notice, she was pleased with it.

"If the words *Follow The Heron* mean anything to you, come and see me at Le Blanc Cellars," she read out loud as she held the page up in front of her. "Ha!" she cheered. "This is ridiculous, but it just might work!"

She read it through a couple more times before placing it carefully on the passenger seat of her car and making her way to the park. She smiled the entire way as she drove. She was impressed with her plan and certain that it would yield results that would force Charles and the entire police force to eat their words.

You're his boss. You could just instruct him to believe you, and he'd have to do it...no, that would be stupid. Why do you care so much about what Charles thinks? She forced the question from her mind. It had been replaying for hours, and she didn't want to take the time to determine the answer. Mainly because she was certain the answer was a reality that she was not yet ready to face.

～

Avery scanned the notice board at the festival to find the perfect spot for her poster. She wondered first how many people actually looked at the board. She knew that she hadn't looked at it once since the festival began. Most of what was up there were advertisements for music lessons or snake removals, things of that nature. Her notice would seem completely out of place. But perhaps that was best.

She was about to pin the page to the board when another thought crossed her mind. *What if the police see this? Could I get into any kind of trouble?* Avery scanned the field around her, looking for any sign of their blue uniform. She took her time, too. She wanted to be absolutely certain that no police officer saw her putting the sign up. When she was certain the coast was completely clear, she neatly pinned the sign to the board.

She took a step back, admiring her work. She'd printed the letters in bright red, similar to those that had been written on the stones, and the words *Follow The Heron* were in bold. A wide smile crossed her face as she read through it a few more times.

"And now we wait," she said quietly.

At that moment, a familiar voice called out to her. It was Tiffany. Avery swung around to find the source of the voice and spotted Tiffany waving at her from the line at the coffee cart.

"Can I buy you a cup?" Tiffany asked as Avery approached to greet her.

"Oh, please, I'm dying for another cup," Avery answered cheerfully.

They waited together until they had their cups of coffee. Avery was about to sip hers when an unexpected and intrusive thought popped into her head. *What if he'd been poisoned by the coffee?* She hesitated for a moment, but when the rich aroma of the dark roast coffee filled her lungs, she decided it was worth the risk and eagerly took a large sip.

"Has the mayor been by your stall yet?" Tiffany asked.

Avery shook her head. "No, I haven't seen him at the festival at all," she answered.

"Hmmm," Tiffany responded. "That's odd. He's never missed a year. Do you think he's maybe ill?"

Avery shrugged. She didn't know, and she didn't care. The mayor's presence at the festival meant little to her. As long as she was making sales, she didn't really care.

Hours had passed and every time somebody approached the Le Blanc Cellars stall, Avery got excited. She kept waiting for one of them to say that they knew about the stones or that they had some information she was looking for.

But they all just took their sips of wine and left. With the overcast weather threatening to rain them out, it was a particularly quiet day at the festival. The crowd was small, and most of the people who attended were only there to socialize. So, sales were low too.

The time moved by slowly as she waited for someone to come and give her the information she needed to prove Charles wrong. Eventually, she felt like she should simply give up, pack up her stall, and call it for the day. It was by far the quietest day they'd had since the festival started. But then it dawned on her. What exactly was she expecting them to say? If they did, in fact, have any information, why would they be willing to share it with her?

That's when an even more terrifying thought danced around in her mind. *What if the stones really are part of the murder? Now I've put up a sign that practically tells the world I know about it. Will they poison me next?*

A wave of nausea washed over her as she thought about it even further. It had been so foolish of her to think something like that might have worked. She could have gotten herself into heaps of trouble, not only with the police but with the actual murderer.

The whole thought of it made her dizzy, and she rushed over to the notice board. She ripped the sign off, hoping nobody had seen her doing it, and stuffed it in her pocket.

"What were you thinking?" she whispered as she walked back in the direction of her stall.

By the time she made it back to pour the next wine tasting for the newest eager visitor, she had decided without a doubt that it had been entirely Charles' fault. He was the reason that she was being so foolish about it all.

If he had just agreed with her and taken her side, then she wouldn't have been so determined to prove him wrong. Avery knew it was unreasonable to put the blame on Charles, but it made her feel better.

Then, it only made her more upset.

How dare he push me so far that I do something so daft? It was an absurd thought, and she knew it. And yet, it made sense to her. Charles was the reason she was behaving this way. If he had only done a better job of supporting her beliefs, she would have slept better, behaved better, and probably made more sales that day. That's how she felt, anyway.

Chapter Five

The coffee shop was packed, and Avery was having a hard time speaking over the noise of the crowd. It had been years since the town had been that busy, and Avery and Tiffany had walked all over just to find a restaurant with a table available for them.

Inside the restaurant, music was filtering evenly. The entire space was filled with green plants, and the smell of coffee hung in the air. It made Avery feel relaxed, and she was happy for a little bit of privacy among the plants. She could catch Tiffany up on everything that had happened.

"Where did you find the other two stones?" Tiffany asked in horror as she listened eagerly to Avery's story.

"On the outskirts of the park; that's why everyone seems to think it's just coincidence or whatever," Avery answered between mouthfuls of her delicious lunch. "If you ask me, it's the furthest thing from a coincidence."

"You know he's just doing his job, right?" Tiffany asked. "He's acting like a police officer."

"That's fine," Avery said. "But he's supposed to be my friend too. Couldn't he just take my side this one time?"

"He's always been on your side," Tiffany laughed. "Honestly, I don't know why this has you so upset."

"I don't know either," Avery sighed. "I guess I just think there's more to this than they want to admit. It doesn't make sense for it to be a coincidence."

"It doesn't make sense at all, in any sense," Tiffany agreed.

"Do you think I've overreacted a little?" Avery frowned as she reached for her coffee. "I haven't spoken to Charles again since."

"Maybe a little," Tiffany said with a shrug. "But that's normal. You care about each other, and you wanted him to hear you out. I get it."

We care about each other.

Tiffany was absolutely correct. Avery cared too much about what Charles thought. That's why she had been so upset. It should have been obvious to her, but it wasn't. She just wanted him to take her seriously, and when he didn't, it made her feel foolish.

Why doesn't he just listen to me? Surely he doesn't think that I am too stupid to understand it all? We've known each other some time now, at the very least, you'd think he'd properly look into it for me.

She was about to voice this revelation when Tiffany suddenly spotted something to her left and pointed at it with her knife. "Isn't that the guy's wife? The one that was crying so much? She was screaming like mad, remember?"

Avery brushed past the insensitivity in Tiffany's voice and glanced over to where she had been pointing. Tiffany was right. The dead man's wife was sitting at a table not too far from them. She paged through a design magazine, flipping cheerfully through the pages. Then, she received a phone call and answered it. Avery watched in awe as the woman joked and laughed with whoever was on the other end of the call.

"She seems a little too cheerful for someone who just lost her husband," Avery commented. "I mean, now isn't the time to be cracking jokes."

"Maybe that's how she copes? With jokes and stuff," Tiffany said.

"Trust me," Avery whispered. "I've been where she is. Nothing is funny when you've just lost the love of your life."

Tiffany cast her eyes downward and put her knife back down on her plate. "You're right; I'm sorry," she said.

Avery looked back at the woman who continued to flip through the magazine while she spoke on the phone. From what Avery could hear, she was discussing an upcoming holiday to the Maldives. The entire scenario made Avery's blood run cold. Nothing about it seemed normal or right to her.

The woman then lifted her hand and pushed her sleek blonde hair off her neck and over her shoulder, revealing a tattoo on the back of her neck. Avery stared at it for a while. She could make out the shape of two wings that wrapped around the back of the woman's neck.

"It's a heron," Tiffany said sternly. "Look."

"No, surely not," Avery said with an uneasy chuckle. "It could be any kind of bird, honestly."

"Look closer; I'm telling you it's a heron," Tiffany pressed.

Avery narrowed her eyes in an attempt to focus on the tattoo. But she knew that Tiffany was right. The dead man's wife had a large tattoo of a heron on the back of her neck. That could not possibly be a coincidence.

What Avery felt was a mix of excitement and panic. She had stumbled onto information that was potentially groundbreaking to the case, and it made her feel bad for the dead man. Then again, it was enough to prove Charles wrong.

"What do we do with this?" Tiffany asked. "Do we go to the police? Should we call Charles?"

"I don't know. We need to know more before we accuse her of anything," Avery said. "Let's run this past the Stammtisch."

"I'm on it."

Tiffany was the newest member of the Stammtisch, and the group had only gotten closer over the last few months. They were a group of women who all loved wine and had very few things in common, but they got together regularly and had a good time anyway.

A few hours later, Avery's living room was filled with the group of women, who listened eagerly as she filled them all in on what had happened.

It was the classic, perfect mix of characters. Eleanor was the founder of the group. She was feisty and had no problem speaking her mind. Deb, married to a wealthy vineyard owner, spent most of her day visiting with friends. She was a walking tabloid for anything that was happening in the town. Camille was often present, but most of the time, her mind was somewhere else. Still, she joined in when it seemed to count. Tiffany was the newest in the group. She was Avery's childhood friend, and she just seemed happy that she had a reason to be social.

"Why haven't you told Charles yet?" Eleanor asked. "About the lady and her tattoo?"

"Well," Avery searched for the right answer. "He's working at my stall at the festival today, and I need more proof. I mean, we only think it was a heron on the back of her neck. It could have been a crane or something."

"Pfft," Deb scoffed. "Please, Avery, you know better. You need to trust your gut."

"I'm pretty sure it's a heron," Tiffany added.

"Well, I just think I need to be absolutely sure, and besides, I want to slam some really solid evidence in Charles' face. I can't wait to see his reaction," Avery said excitedly.

"Why do you care so much about what he thinks?" Camille asked. "Just go tell him, and let the police do their jobs."

"I have to agree with Avery," Tiffany stepped in. "Before we accuse the woman of being involved in her husband's death, let's just be sure about it first."

The women spent the next few hours going through all sorts of possibilities in excruciating detail. They discussed her body language at the restaurant while one of them googled what it all meant. They looked up photographs of herons as Avery and Tiffany tried desperately to remember the details of the tattoo.

"What was she like when she learned of her husband's death?" Eleanor asked.

"She was screaming and crying and on the ground," Avery said, exasperated at that point.

"Crying?" Eleanor asked. "Were there any real tears? Or did she just look like she was crying?"

Avery thought about it for a while. "Now that you mention it, I saw her scream and put up a fairly decent fight against the police. But then, she just stopped and let them take her away."

"But were there actual wet tears, though?" Eleanor asked again.

"Honestly," Avery answered. "I was a little too distracted by the dead guy to be paying close enough attention."

The sun was already setting when one of them finally asked. "So what should we do about this?"

"We need to gather more information, but where do we start?" Eleanor answered.

"We don't even know where to find her," Deb added.

The group of women fell silent for a moment as they all thought it over. Avery enjoyed the brief moment of silence; it had been a busy few days, and she was tired.

"The festival," Avery finally clicked. "Tomorrow is the last day...the day of the auction. Everybody goes to the auction."

"You're right!" Eleanor cheered. "We'll all go and keep an eye out for her. If we spot her, we wait until she leaves and follow her to know where she is staying."

"That's an excellent idea!" Camille agreed.

With that, it was decided. The group of women would have their own little top-secret operation. Once one of them had determined where the woman was staying, they would let Avery know. She would then go and speak to the woman, offering her support and condolences. Hopefully, she would be invited in for coffee, and then she could get as much information about the woman as possible and ask about the tattoo on the back of her neck. She would then be able to take that information and rub it in Charles' face.

There was still so much that didn't make sense to Avery. She thought about how her late husband would write his crime novels. There was just too much missing information when it came to the woman with the heron tattoo that she couldn't seem to piece together anything logical. For one thing, there was no motive. Unhappy marriages end in divorce, not murder. Still, she knew she was on the verge of getting the information she needed.

That night, she struggled to fall asleep. She spent most of the night fantasizing over all the ways she might take the evidence she was certain she'd gather and show it to Charles. She imagined what his face might look like when he learned that she was right and he was wrong.

She hadn't spoken to him again since the phone call

about the stones. Some part of her missed him through all of this. He had a way of guiding her to the right answer—even when she didn't want to hear it.

The women of the Stammtisch were a great support, but they easily got carried away, and they were a lot of energy to deal with all at once. At least when she went to Charles, he was always calm, quiet, and eager to listen.

But still, the way he'd so easily taken somebody else's side had her unreasonably upset. Their plan had been solidified, and she knew exactly what to do. The next time she spoke to Charles, she'd have a little more than just speculation, and she'd hopefully convince him to believe her.

In the meantime, she would take instruction from some stones and follow the heron.

Chapter Six

It was a beautiful sunny day when Avery opened her eyes again. With a plan of action, she found it easier to drag her tired body out of bed and get prepared for the day. That evening was the auction, and she was determined to follow through with their plan. There was only one thing that she was nervous about. She needed to figure out what exactly she would say to the lady with the heron tattoo when she got the chance. She knew she needed to somehow get something out of her that would pass as evidence.

But what would that be exactly? Perhaps she only needed to prove that the woman wasn't all too sad about her husband's passing at all. She wasn't sure yet, but she needed to come up with something. If the woman really was involved, she couldn't say anything that would make it obvious that she knew about it. That could put her own life in danger or the woman could simply skip town, and the entire thing would be a bust.

It felt as if she was on one of her favorite crime shows or perhaps part of one of her late husband's crime novels. Part of it was exciting, but it mostly made her nervous. She would have preferred to have no part in it, but she was far too stubborn for that.

By the time the evening rolled in, and the auction had begun, Avery still didn't know what she would say, but she had run out of time. At any minute, the lady with the heron tattoo would make an appearance, and the plan would be set in motion.

She couldn't concentrate on anything else as she scanned the sea of people over and over again, looking for the woman. She realized that it might be more difficult than she'd anticipated. Everyone had dressed up for the auction, and she wasn't entirely confident she knew what the woman's face looked like.

Without the heron tattoo visible, she couldn't even be certain if she had the right woman at all. If the woman had her hair down, how would they know it was her? These were all things they had not considered when they had made the plan, and it was only making Avery more nervous.

The auction had turned out to be a rather extravagant event. The section of the park where the auction was being held had been decorated with balloons and red velvet chairs. There were waiters carrying trays with wine and bubbly. It seemed to be the event of the year. To one side, a violinist in a flashy black dress covered in sequins played smooth jazz. There had even been a makeshift cigar lounge set up in one place with large leather sofas and a Persian rug.

As she looked through the crowd, she spotted the women of the Stammtisch also glancing through the auction attendees. They were sticking to the plan.

Who knows? Maybe I'll get lucky, and she'll have her hair up. Avery took a deep breath and tried to stay as focused as possible. She walked around the back of the crowd, slowly inspecting every blonde woman she could spot. Most of them she knew, so that took them out of the lineup automatically.

Later, after the auction, it was time for everyone to socialize. Then, it became even more difficult to look for the woman with the heron tattoo. People mingled and walked around each other constantly. Many people stopped Avery to have a conversation with her, drawing her attention away from the task at hand.

By the end of the evening, the ladies were all defeated. It seemed that the woman with the heron tattoo never made an appearance. This meant that their plan had not worked, and since it was their one and only plan, she no longer knew what to do. Which, in turn, meant that she'd have to go to the police and Charles, tell them about the heron tattoo, and hope that they'd see it the way that she did.

Just to be certain, Avery waited at the sidelines as everyone left the field, hoping that perhaps she'd simply missed the woman. But by the time Avery was the last one standing, it had become clear that there was no hope.

The lights that hovered above the festivities were switched off, tables and banners were packed up, one final cleanup was done throughout the park, and the festival officially came to an end.

To Avery, it was a bittersweet moment. It had been a successful festival. But she had hoped to be able to take the days following to relax and simply enjoy the quiet time. Instead, she knew that she'd be agonizing over the dead man and his wife with the heron tattoo.

When she got home, she poured herself a generous glass of wine and fixed herself a plate of hot food. On her own, she celebrated the success of it all. Le Blanc Cellars had done really well in festival sales, the guesthouse was still fully booked for a few more nights, and the business was generally a success.

Her home was her favorite place on Earth. She'd spent weeks decluttering it of anything that had belonged to previous owners or her parents who had lived in the house before her. She had bought decorative items to make it feel more like her own place. Avery had rearranged almost every piece of furniture until the spaces were barely recognizable. At home, she hid away from the rest of the world and was allowed to do whatever she wanted. This mostly consisted of eating, reading, and watching movies.

It felt odd to celebrate alone, but the only person she felt she should celebrate with was Charles, and she still hadn't spoken to him. She wouldn't know what to talk to him about other than the woman with the heron tattoo, and if he didn't react the way she wanted him to, it would only have made things worse.

After her wine and meal, she got ready for bed but not before checking her phone. She saw a few text messages. Some were from her parents, telling her about the latest political and sports news. There were messages on the Stammtisch group thread saying nobody had spotted the heron tattoo. There was also a message from Charles. She considered, for a moment, ignoring the message but found herself clicking on the chat anyway. Thankfully, the message was positive.

Excellent work! The festival was a great success. You should be proud.

She was about to respond when she saw another message come through from Camille. It was late, and she had just caught the first words when the message popped up at the top of the screen. It was enough to catch Avery's attention, and she switched instead to the chat with Camille.

I found her.

The message was followed by a location pin. Avery's heart skipped a beat. She was so certain that the woman hadn't attended the auction. A few messages back and forth with Camille answered all of her questions.

Avery learned that Camille had spotted the woman grabbing takeout at a local restaurant. She followed her back to where she was staying and immediately texted Avery. She wasted no time letting the rest of the Stammtisch women know that the woman with the heron tattoo had been found.

Then, Avery found herself opening the chat with Charles again. She felt that she had to respond to him somehow. But she didn't know what to say. She typed message after message, only to delete each and every one of them.

In the end, she just closed the chat and said nothing. She knew it wasn't the right thing to do and it likely might upset him. She just needed to wait a little while longer until she had gotten enough out of the woman with the heron tattoo to talk to Charles again. Without it, she knew that she might snap at him, and she really didn't want to hurt his feelings. She didn't want to put him in an uncomfortable situation either if she pressured him about the three stones that were linked to the murder case.

For a while, she did her best to sleep. But it was no use. There was too much on her mind, and she was too excited. Instead, she watched movie after movie in an attempt to speed up time until she eventually fell asleep on the couch with Sprinkles pressed tightly against her legs.

Chapter Seven

Avery and Tiffany parked the car just across the street and a few doors down from where the woman with the heron tattoo was apparently staying. It was a pleasant night, and Avery couldn't help but think she would rather be at home, sipping wine out by the garden. Instead, she was sitting uncomfortably in her car, waiting for something to happen. It seemed silly, but she was stubborn and determined to prove herself right.

"What will you even say to her?" Tiffany asked. "It just seems odd. I mean, I get why we're doing it, but where do you even start?"

"I've been wondering the same thing," Avery answered. "What exactly are we trying to get from her? What would be good enough evidence?"

The two women were clearly not qualified to be staking out any person or home, yet they would both see it through to the end.

"Maybe you just need to find out more about what their relationship was like?" Tiffany suggested. "If she tells you it wasn't a happy marriage, then you have a motive. Wouldn't that be enough?"

"I don't know," Avery said. "Let me think about it. I don't think I'll get any answers soon, though. I might have to just wing it once I get in there."

"That's if you can get her to let you in."

Tiffany was right, and Avery felt like she was in way over her head.

"We don't know if she's the actual one that did it, but I do think she's involved," Avery added. "The stones only said to follow the heron, not that she did it."

"Still," Tiffany said quietly. "She might have done it."

Avery didn't want to think about that too much, considering she would have to go and have a conversation with the woman and hopefully convince her to let Avery into her home.

"Should I have brought binoculars or something?" Avery asked quietly.

"Binoculars?" Tiffany asked. "What on Earth for? I thought you were just going to talk to the woman!"

"I don't know," Avery laughed. "I have no idea what I'm doing!"

Now that they were there and actually watching the woman's house, it occurred to Avery that they might be breaking a bunch of laws themselves. If they got caught, she was certain that they could be charged for something. She was only moments away from calling the entire plan off when Tiffany's eyes lit up.

"Wait! There she is!" Tiffany said, pointing at the house where the woman was staying.

The woman walked to her car. She was dressed up in a short dress with high heels. She had her makeup done and her hair up, exposing the tattoo on the back of her neck. She was not dressed for a quiet night at home and most certainly not dressed like a grieving widow.

Avery was certain that by now, the woman would have heard from the police that her husband's death was a murder. It should be a devastating blow to any woman. It required sweatpants and an oversized shirt, not a form-fitting dress and stilettos.

"Where do you think she's going dressed like that?" Tiffany asked.

"I don't know. But I think we should follow her."

They waited for the woman to get ahead a little before turning on their car. Keeping their distance, they followed her through the streets of the town until they stopped at a gas station.

"She didn't dress up to get gas, I can promise you that," Tiffany joked.

They waited a while until they spotted her leaving again. Then, they followed her a little further through the town.

The town was fairly quiet after the festival. Most of the tourists had already left, and those who were residents were likely resting. It was easy to follow her, and they had little risk of losing her, so they were able to keep their distance.

"This feels a little silly, doesn't it?" Tiffany eventually asked. "I feel like I'm in a detective show, like those on television."

"I know," Avery laughed. "We're being absolutely ridiculous. But I don't know what else to do."

"I should have brought some coffee. I didn't think it was going to take this long," Tiffany teased.

"We'll stop for some wine when this is over. I'm sure I'll need it," Avery promised.

"If we ever find ourselves in this situation again, promise me you'll pack some snacks," Tiffany said.

The two women laughed at the thought. Avery hoped

with every fiber in her being that they would never find themselves following a suspect in a murder case through the small streets of their hometown ever again.

Then again, too many strange things had happened since she moved back from the city. She couldn't guarantee that it wouldn't happen again.

"Do you know what's been bothering me?" Tiffany asked.

Avery shrugged. "I'm no mind reader," she answered sarcastically.

"Do you remember when that man bumped you? And it spilled all the wine?" she asked.

"You mean the dead guy?" Avery laughed. "A little hard to forget."

"Well, do you remember what he was saying when he fell? He was rambling on about something, saying that *she* had done it," Tiffany continued.

"I vaguely remember that," Avery replied. "I think I was too upset about my blouse."

"Well, don't you think that's some evidence right there?" Tiffany said. "Think about it. He rambles on about this *she* that has supposedly *done* something. Then, a few hours later, he's found dead."

"I think I see where you're going with this," Avery mumbled.

"So, what if he didn't fall because he was drunk like we originally thought?" Tiffany continued. "What if he fell because he was poisoned, and he was trying to tell everyone who had done it?"

The thought made Avery's blood run cold. She gripped the steering wheel hard as she thought about it. Tiffany was right. He might have been trying to tell them what was going on, and everyone had simply treated him like a drunk tourist.

It was a terrible thought. Perhaps the man was trying to ask for help. Who knows how difficult it might be to actually talk when there is poison in your blood? She didn't like that thought one bit.

"I feel terrible," Avery said as they rounded another corner.

"Me too," Tiffany said. "I can't imagine what that must have been like for him."

"How awful," Avery whispered. "He might have been a nuisance, but he still deserves justice," Avery said. "We need to get this evidence so we can make this right."

"She's stopping," Tiffany said. "Isn't that the mayor's house?"

They stopped a few houses down and turned off their lights. Avery was no expert in following others, but she'd watched enough crime shows to know she needed to turn the lights of her car off if she didn't want to be spotted.

They watched as the woman with the heron tattoo spent a moment in the car fixing her hair and makeup. Everything about her behavior was odd to Avery. She couldn't quite figure out what the woman was doing.

"What is she doing?" Tiffany asked.

"I don't know. But I don't have a good feeling about this."

When the woman finally stepped out of the car, they noticed a bottle of red wine sticking out of her purse. Avery knew from the seal on top of the bottle that it was a red wine from Le Blanc Cellars. She hated the idea that a woman who was potentially involved in the murder of her own husband would favor the wine from her winery.

She rang the doorbell at the mayor's house.

"You can see the tattoo pretty well. Maybe you should take a photograph," Tiffany suggested.

Avery hurried to get her phone out of her bag and

zoomed in as far as she could. She had the woman's head and shoulders in the frame and was about to take a photograph when the mayor pulled the door open. Avery snapped the photo just as the mayor pressed his lips to the woman's.

The two women gasped loudly as they watched the situation unfold in front of them.

"Hardly seems like a grieving widow to me," Tiffany said.

The kiss was no ordinary old-people-greeting-kiss either. Neither of them was old enough to warrant one of those, and it lingered for a solid few seconds before the mayor snuggled into the nape of her neck.

"Please tell me you got that on camera," Tiffany said with a hint of excitement in her voice.

"You bet I did. I got a great shot." She presented Tiffany with an image of the woman and the mayor kissing, with the tattoo clearly in view.

"Ha!" Tiffany cheered. "Busted!" Tiffany's excitement quickly fell, and a frown crossed her face. "That scoundrel," she mumbled.

The women sped off, leaving the mayor and the tattooed woman in the distance. Avery wasn't sure if the mayor had spotted them leaving, but she didn't care. She had enough evidence to give the woman a solid motive, prove herself right, and prove Charles and the police wrong.

She felt odd for feeling so smug about it, but she didn't care. She simply needed people to know that there was more to her than meets the eye and that the next time she came with what she felt was important information, they should take it more seriously.

"I'm too excited to sleep," Tiffany said when Avery dropped her back home. "I know it sounds ridiculous because we're talking about the death of a man here, but maybe I should change careers. Suddenly, being a cop sounds like fun."

Avery laughed. "Don't get ahead of yourself. You forget how bored we were for eighty percent of that experience."

She told her best friend goodnight and headed home. Avery's head was swimming with theories and thoughts that she had no control over. Then, a familiar sinking feeling hit the pit of her stomach.

What if the woman wasn't simply involved somehow? What if she is the murderer? What if they saw your car leave? What if they recognize your car and know that you've seen them? What have you gotten yourself into, Avery?

Chapter Eight

The vineyard was dead quiet, and the only source of light came from Avery's living room. There, she scrolled between the photographs, admiring every detail of them. She relived the events of the night over and over in her mind, trying to comprehend it all.

It had been a remarkably successful stakeout. She felt as if she were watching one of her late husband's crime novels playing out right in front of her eyes. She had been like one of his characters that night, and the adrenaline had not yet worn off.

It was a little before midnight when Avery eventually reached for her phone and sent Charles the photographs. She had intended to wait a while before showing them to him, but she couldn't sleep and didn't want to wait any longer. There were too many thoughts plaguing her mind, and she couldn't keep them all to herself any longer. Once the photos were sent, she got up and headed for bed. Her plan was to sleep so that she could speed up time. She had assumed that Charles would only see them in the morning, but a few minutes later, her phone rang.

"I assume you got the photographs," she answered.

"What the hell is this?" he asked.

That was it. There was no greeting, no excitement from him. Instead, he sounded annoyed. Avery had never heard him talk to her like that before, and she didn't enjoy it one bit.

"I took them myself, if you must know," she said. "Did you see the tattoo?"

"Yes, it's a bird. Is that the mayor?"

He spoke to her the same way her teachers had spoken to her in school when she just didn't understand the lesson.

"It's a *heron*," Avery said quite proudly. "So, I followed it. Just like the stones suggested." It sounded ridiculous when she said it out loud and not nearly as cool as she thought it would, which caused the frustration to build and created a small localized headache on the left side of her head. She raised two fingers to her temple and massaged her head in a circular motion.

There was a brief silence on the other end of the line. A part of her hoped that he wouldn't say anything else. But she knew that it was wishful thinking.

"You didn't answer my question," he said. "Is that the mayor?"

Avery sighed. "Yes, that is the mayor...who is quite clearly in a relationship with the dead guy's wife. If you ask me, that's a motive for murder." Avery smiled. She felt quite pleased about it all. She was certain that Charles would be grateful for the evidence. They didn't have a lot of time to solve the murder before the victim's body was supposed to be returned to his hometown. Now, she could help them somehow.

"Avery, please tell me you didn't sneak outside the mayor's house and take photographs of him without his consent." Charles almost sounded like he was begging; he was so desperate for it not to be true. And Avery hadn't looked at it that way. She had just assumed that she was doing the right thing and wanted to shove it in Charles' face.

"I guess when you put it that way, it doesn't sound too good."

"I don't have to tell you that it is illegal to do that without the necessary paperwork. Surely you know that? You're not a police officer, Avery. Why didn't you tell me that you were going to do this? I would have advised you against it."

Avery sighed. "You didn't even believe me that the stones had anything to do with the case in the first place. Why would you have believed me about this?"

"It's not that I didn't believe you, Avery. It was just that the police officers made a good point. At the time, there was no reason to believe the stones were all that relevant to solving the case," he explained. "But if you had told me that you found the victim's wife with a heron tattoo, I definitely would have suggested that they look into it."

"Well, I saved you the trouble," Avery said proudly.

"What if you had been caught?"

Avery couldn't believe it. He was still arguing with her about it. Better yet, he was upset about something that might have happened but didn't. So, he was really upset about absolutely nothing.

"I didn't get caught, though," she said smugly. "And you're welcome, by the way."

"I can't do anything with this, Avery," he said. By that point, it sounded as if he wanted to shout from frustration. "If I send this to the police officers, they're going to ask me where I got it from, and you'll immediately be in trouble. Besides, you're going in the wrong direction."

"Not according to the stones," she said, feeling smug.

"It's precisely the stones that I'm referring to," he explained. "We found where they probably came from."

"Oh?"

"They're a type of pond stone," he said. "There's one shop here that sells them, and apparently they've only ever sold them to one person. The postman."

"So is he a suspect?" she asked.

"Yes, and the police would love to look into him," Charles said, annoyed. "But all this with the mayor is a problem, Avery. You've really made a mess now."

Avery didn't know how to respond. She understood what she did was wrong, but she never realized that it might have been for nothing. She just wanted to show off to Charles and prove to him that it was worth taking her seriously. Instead, by doing that, she had interfered with a case, and none of it even made a difference.

"Alright," Charles eventually said after a long silence. "This is good evidence, Avery. It needs to be sent to the police, but they can't know it came from you."

Avery smiled a little. "So what do we do?"

"You can put in an anonymous tip with these photographs. I'll send you all the information on how to do it."

"That's a great idea," she said hopefully. "So then it isn't all for nothing? Do you think they'll arrest her or something?"

"I don't know," Charles said through a loud and annoyed sigh. "But if this doesn't work, and they discover that we both have seen the photographs...Avery, if they know you took this, and that I knew about it and didn't say anything... It's not that the police would do anything, but the mayor could take legal action against both of us."

"Do you think he'd do that?" she asked foolishly.

"Wouldn't you?" he snapped. "Please tell me that you understand how reckless this was?"

"Yessss, Charles," Avery whined as she rolled her eyes.

"Why didn't you just tell me?" he asked again, this time with more desperation in his voice. "You haven't spoken to me in days. Is this what you've been up to?"

"Well, yes and no," she answered. "There's been the festival. I suppose me and the girls did spend about two days on this plan," she admitted.

"You and the girls?"

"Yeah, the ladies from the Stammtisch. They helped me track down where she was staying."

Charles let out his longest, breathiest sigh yet. Avery could hear him grinding his teeth on the other end of the call. "Just hope none of them talk about the photographs around town because then it will certainly lead back to you," he said.

"Not all of them know about the mayor yet. Only Tiffany. She was with me," Avery said.

"Well, tell her to keep quiet about it," he snapped. "She's a smart girl; she'll understand how illegal this is."

Avery frowned. Had Charles implied that she wasn't smart? After all, she hadn't considered the legalities of it until Charles had mentioned it only a few minutes earlier. Her cheeks got warm as she started to get angry again.

"Alright, I'll tell her. So, what do I do now?" she asked, unable to hide the irritation in her voice.

"Don't worry about it. I've thought about it some more, and I'll send the anonymous tip for you. I'll keep you posted if anything happens or we've been found out," he said.

"And what about the postman?" she asked.

"Oh no," he said. "I'm not giving you any more information about this. You'll only get involved and cause me even more trouble."

Without saying goodbye or goodnight, Charles hung up the phone. Avery couldn't believe it. He no longer trusted her at all. He didn't even think she could handle putting in an anonymous tip. How hard could it be?

Still, her conversation with him had made her feel nervous. He was right. She had essentially stalked a woman and taken inappropriate photographs of the mayor. What was she thinking? How had she allowed herself to become so irrational?

After a couple of cups of tea and a few hours of thinking it over, she decided it was Charles' fault. He was the one who had made her so irrational. Avery hadn't quite worked out why she had reacted so extremely, but she was satisfied that he was at fault.

With that, she climbed into bed and rolled around for hours, agonizing over all the ways she could have handled their conversation differently.

When morning finally came around and the vineyard came to life, she dragged her near-zombie body out of bed. Avery could feel the bags under her eyes every time she blinked and did her best not to cry when she saw her exhausted reflection in the mirror.

She was so consumed with trying to get her concealer right that she almost completely ignored the sound of her phone buzzing. However, when she saw Charles' name out of the corner of her eye, she dropped everything she was doing to read the message.

Anonymous tip was well-received. They're bringing her in for questioning. Don't forget—nobody can know it was you.

Avery was so pleased that she did a little dance to celebrate. She was right, and that was all that mattered. The stones had indeed meant something, and now there was proof of it. As she turned to face her reflection again, she wondered if Charles had slept at all.

She imagined him staring at his own tired, stressed-out reflection in the mirror, and her heart dropped. She had caused him a lot of trouble, and he had every right to be upset with her. Yet, she felt that she was the one who deserved to be angry, simply because he didn't react exactly the way she would have liked him to.

Avery understood better the arguments that she and her mother had when she was growing up. When her mother had expected her to be apologetic, she had been unbothered. Those were the biggest fights her family had ever had.

It turned out she was more like her mother than she'd hoped.

Chapter Nine

No amount of pacing or distractions could stop her mind from agonizing over it all. She had gone to the wine room to speak to Charles and see how he was doing, but he seemed entirely uninterested in having a conversation with her. He had kept it professional, of course, but Avery could see that something was wrong. She had put him in a difficult position, and she didn't like the idea of that one bit, but couldn't he just forgive her? She wanted them to joke and tease like they used to.

She didn't have time to think about any of it anymore. That night was the barbecue social event for everyone who had taken part in the festival. Charles would be there, and at first, Avery had thought maybe they could travel together. But she didn't think it was worth asking him anymore.

So, she slipped on her best barbecue dress and waited for the taxi to arrive to take her.

The event was pretty uneventful. There were people talking in small groups. The men gathered around the fire like moths while some of the women chatted about salads.

Avery couldn't help but notice that no matter where she was in the space, Charles was on the opposite side.

There was light jazz playing and fine wine all around. For the most part, the wine was all that got Avery's attention. Everyone had gotten together to celebrate the success of the festival. Avery was about to call the taxi to take her home when she spotted a familiar face arrive at the barbecue.

The mayor walked in hours late. He looked exhausted as if he'd had a particularly tough day, and Avery was sure she knew why. *Probably took you by surprise when they came to arrest your girlfriend.*

Despite her better knowledge, Avery found herself approaching the mayor rather confidently. "Mayor Oswald," she said. "It's lovely to see you here. My name is Avery, from Le Blanc Cellars."

The mayor flashed her a bright smile. "It's lovely to meet you, Avery. Your Chenin Blanc is my favorite, I must admit."

"I'm so pleased to hear that," Avery said, doing her best to sound as friendly as possible. "You're a little pale. Are you alright?"

He was going to answer, but Avery didn't give him the opportunity.

"You know, I was expecting to see more of you at the festival. I was worried that perhaps you would be ill."

"Ah, yes," the mayor said. "I believe this year's festival has been one of the most successful yet!"

"You know who else I noticed was missing?" she continued. "The postman. He's such a friendly man, I was hoping to get the chance to speak with him and get to know him."

She knew how ridiculous it sounded, but she couldn't get the idea of the postman being a murderer out of her head. He was a perfect criminal. He knew enough about everyone in the town to know what their weaknesses were.

If it were one of her husband's books, he'd definitely have been the kind of character to get away with murder.

"Well, luckily for you, he's a friend of mine," the mayor answered. "I'll let him know to knock on your door next time he delivers the post, and the two of you can chat."

At that moment, someone decided they wanted to make the fourth toast for the evening. Avery wanted to kick herself. She should have just left when she was going to. Now, she had to suffer through yet another thank-you speech and cheerleading session for the upcoming year.

She was exhausted, and all she wanted to do was sleep, but she couldn't tear herself away from the opportunity for a conversation with the mayor. Besides, Charles still wasn't talking to her, so she didn't have many other people to talk to.

Almost ten minutes later, when the speech was finally concluded, Avery turned immediately back to the mayor. She knew by the look in his eyes that he wanted to leave just as badly as she did and that he was in no mood to talk with her. She wanted to see exactly how much information he would give her, though, and how much information he knew.

"Would you like to walk with me?" she offered. "I heard that there is a lovely duck pond at the end of the property. Besides, between you and me, I'm afraid they might start another speech." Avery chuckled. The mayor checked the level of the wine in his glass, looked despairingly at the group of people, and agreed.

"Yes, the festival has been excellent. The best sales we've had in years. I look forward to the next one," Avery said.

"That's good news!" the mayor said, forcing a cheerful tone.

Avery had always pitied people that had gone into politics. She'd always felt that she wasn't a good enough actor for it. She had a problem where her thoughts would often be accurately displayed on her face.

Politicians didn't have that problem. They had a manner of speaking which could make bad news seem like something worth celebrating. She recognized that same tone in the mayor's voice as they walked slowly across the grass.

The sound of the barbecue was growing quieter in the distance.

"It's just a tragedy about the dead tourist," she said, choosing her words carefully.

"Yes," the mayor said. "I've heard all about it. I believe the police are doing the best they can."

"So what's it like being friends with the postman?" she asked, pretending it excited her. "He must have so much information on all of us."

"Well, if he does, then he doesn't say," he answered. "In fact, I had dinner with him just the other night, and he hardly mentioned any of the townsfolk at all."

"I'm part of a stammtisch, and let me tell you, we discuss all of you all of the time," Avery joked.

The mayor chuckled. "I must admit, I am a little worried about him. He didn't seem like himself the last time I saw him."

The mayor's statement sent Avery's mind into overdrive.

Perhaps he didn't seem like himself because he was preparing for murder. Still, there was one thing that bothered her. If the stones came from the postman's pond, how did they wind up in the hands of the victim, with a clue scribbled on them?

Avery watched as the mayor's fingers fidgeted nervously with the stem of his wine glass. He kept his eyes downcast as he spoke, putting on yet another performance.

"To think, while the rest of us enjoyed the concert,

singing our hearts out and having a blast, he simply sat on that bench and waited as his final minutes ticked by."

Mayor Oswald stumbled a little at those words but did an excellent job of regaining his balance. Avery was watching him closely, wondering if his body language was a sign of how much he knew or simply just because he was clearly quite tired.

"Unfortunately, I couldn't attend the first day of the festival," he said.

That was a lie. Avery was certain of it. Although it had been brief, she knew she had seen him that day at the festival. She thought back on every minute of that first day, trying to remember every small detail or something she might have missed. It didn't make sense for the mayor to lie about something like that. She had seen him, but where? It had been somewhere odd, that much she could remember. She knew that as fact because she had made a mental note of it.

"That's a pity, I suppose," Avery said. "The poor man's wife. She looked so distraught. The police had to practically drag her away."

Mayor Oswald's expression didn't change, as if his face had been set in plaster. Avery knew instantly that he was trying too hard not to look as if he had any emotion toward the mention of the dead man's wife.

"Yes, I can only imagine," he said in a deadpan voice.

They had finally made it to the end of the path, and the mayor was looking back up at the barbecue as if he suddenly wished he was among the crowd.

"My apologies, Mayor Oswald, I've chosen a rather uncomfortable topic of discussion," she said.

"No, that's not a problem at all," he said with a smile that seemed almost genuine. "I suppose the event is playing on all our minds, and I'm sure everyone has a lot of questions."

"It's an odd thing to have happened at an event like that," Avery said, keeping a close eye on his body language. "But I have faith that you've got it all under control."

In the distance, Avery could hear the sound of yet another fork being tapped against the bell of a wine glass and let out a sigh of relief, knowing that it was a speech she would be lucky enough to miss.

Avery looked out over the pond. The ducks moved slowly over the water, which reflected the light of the moon. In the darkness, she could hear the water as it lapped against the edge of the pond. She closed her eyes and breathed in the fresh air.

"Ducks are peaceful when they're like this," she said. "Other times, they're nippy little creatures."

She looked at the pond and thought about the postman again. She wondered if maybe he did do it. Charles had given her so little information. But what would his motive be?

The mayor chuckled. "I've had my fair share of duck pinches."

"You know, I'd have to say that ducks are not at all my favorite bird," Avery said. "My favorite bird would be something more like a graceful swan...or perhaps a sparrow."

The mayor stared into the water and smiled. "I'm not sure I know many people who would say ducks are their favorite bird."

"I suppose not many people ask that kind of question anymore," Avery chuckled. "It seems like something that children ask each other."

"Well," the mayor said cheerfully. "Perhaps that's what is wrong with the world. Grown-ups have stopped asking about each other's simplest interests."

"I don't follow," Avery said blankly.

"Children get to know each other, you know?" he explained. "And not on a business level, like grown-ups do. Adults want to know what you do for a living, where you plan on traveling next, or how things are going with your great-aunt."

Mayor Oswald looked out over the pond with the ducks. "Children don't care about all those extra things. They just want to know about *you*. They ask about your favorite color, food, or bird," he said.

He wasn't wrong. And Avery suddenly found herself questioning whether or not she knew anybody's favorite color. Or even whether she knew her own, should anybody ever ask her.

"Well, Mayor Oswald," Avery said, turning to face him. "What is your favorite bird?"

The mayor tapped his nail against the side of his glass as he thought about it for a while. Then he perked up as if the answer had suddenly come to him. He smiled at Avery. "My favorite bird would have to be a heron."

Chapter Ten

A heron. Avery couldn't believe that would be his answer. Well, she could believe it. She just didn't want to. Then again, he had no way of knowing that she knew about the heron tattoo. He must have figured it was a safe topic of discussion.

Avery wished that somebody else had been there to hear it. She knew she shouldn't pry any further, but her curious nature was stronger than her self-control.

"Why do you pick a heron?" she asked, trying not to let her excited energy be too apparent in her voice.

"Why do you pick a swan? Or a sparrow?" he asked, challenging her.

Avery thought it over for a moment. If she wanted him to be forthcoming with her, she would need to make him believe that she was being honest with him. To do so, she figured she might as well speak honestly.

"Swans have been my favorite since I was a little girl," she explained. "They used to remind me of ballerinas, and I've always been a terrible dancer. So, I was somewhat jealous of the swans."

Mayor Oswald let out an amused snort. "And the sparrows?"

"The sparrows remind me of my late husband," she answered honestly. "We went away for a week once. It was one of the only times when he wasn't writing toward a deadline. The place where we stayed had a nest full of sparrows. My husband and I sat for hours watching them, doing absolutely nothing. It's a fond memory."

Through the darkness, she was certain that she'd spotted the corners of his mouth turning ever so slightly upward.

"So, why do you pick a heron?" she asked again.

"Well, they do only ever what we expect to see of them. I like the simplicity in that," he answered. "They're graceful creatures...but mostly they remind me of someone important to me."

Avery's heart sank with horror at the same time that her heart fluttered with excitement. She didn't know what to do or say. Grateful for the cover of darkness, she closed her eyes and took a moment to compose herself.

He had no idea that what he was saying to her was dangerous to him. Then again, perhaps it wasn't dangerous to him after all since there were no witnesses to hear what he was saying. *Surely I am a viable witness?*

She couldn't stop then. She needed to find out a little more. Whatever was going on between the mayor, the woman with the heron tattoo, and the dead man was more sinister than anyone had expected, and the mayor was somehow involved.

Avery wanted to know exactly how involved he was and exactly how forthcoming he was expected to be.

"Did you know the man that died?" she asked before realizing that the question came seemingly out of the blue. "Sorry, it seems silly, but I've just realized that I've been talking about it, and perhaps you knew him. That would make it a difficult conversation to have, and I don't want to have crossed any boundaries or stepped on any toes," she continued, recovering only slightly.

"No need to worry," the mayor said calmly. "I didn't know him at all. He was a tourist, I believe."

Avery wasn't entirely satisfied with that answer. It did nothing to quench her curious thirst. Instead, it only left her feeling rather bored with the conversation. "His poor wife," she sighed. "Some of the locals seem to know her. Do you know her at all? The poor thing."

The quacking of the ducks nearby briefly interrupted them, and a small part of Avery wished it would continue on a little longer. She had no idea what the mayor would say, and she had no idea what she really wanted him to say either.

"No, I can't say that I know her. I believe she is quite distraught."

Avery wanted to gasp, but she couldn't. She did feel a little dizzy, though, because she knew the truth, and she hated that he'd lied. She hated even more that she wasn't surprised that he'd lied. She wanted to push him into the pond and let the ducks attack him. She wanted to kick him in the shins and shout at him for being a liar. But everything she knew was supposed to remain anonymous. So, she had to keep quiet. If not for her own security, she had to do it for Charles.

"So, which days were you at the festival?" she asked. "Because I thought I saw you on the first day, but you say that you weren't there. Must have been your doppelganger."

"No, I wasn't there on the first day," he answered.

Once again, she was certain he was lying. Not only that, but he was avoiding her question. She was about to give the mayor a piece of her mind when she decided to rather change the topic of discussion.

"So, what's the postman like?" she asked. "If he knocks on my door, what can I offer to him for tea?"

The mayor shrugged. "The funny thing about our postman is that he really isn't all that friendly," he said. "And still, he is a sensitive creature. He nearly quit his job right before the festival. He said some tourist had been just awful to him. I had to beg him to stay. He's been the best postman we've ever had."

"There you are," Charles said, canceling Avery's opportunity to further her prying. "I was wondering where you disappeared to."

Avery turned to face the origin of the voice and saw the silhouette of Charles, illuminated by the lights from the barbecue.

"You missed some great speeches," he said coyly. "Ah! Mayor Oswald. How good to see you again."

"Hey, Charles," Avery said, unamused. "We came to look at the ducks and get some quiet."

"Yes, that sounds lovely," he said calmly. "But unfortunately, I must let you know that the mayor is expected at the party. It seems they have a gift for you, Mayor Oswald."

The mayor excused himself and made his way back to the festivities, leaving Avery and Charles alone at the duck pond.

"I'm so glad I missed the speeches," she joked. "They can be so tedious, and there were far too many of them. I was afraid that I might be expected to make a speech."

She had taken a step to walk back toward the party when she felt Charles' fingers grip her sleeve, keeping her back. For a brief moment, she wished that he'd taken her hand, but then instantly, the idea made her wish he'd never touched her at all.

"What were you talking to the mayor about?" Charles asked sternly.

"We spoke about the ducks and our favorite birds," she said dryly. "He says his favorite bird is a heron."

"And what else?"

Charles wasn't buying her attempt at downplaying the conversation. She knew he wouldn't approve of it, and she wasn't in the mood for yet another argument with him.

"We spoke about the murder, but he doesn't know that I know it was a murder," she said. "I asked him if he knew the dead man or the man's wife...and a couple of questions about the postman. They're friends."

"You are unbelievable," Charles said as he started walking away from her.

"He lied to me," she argued, following him back up the path. "He said he didn't know either of them. He's willing to hide it all."

Charles spun around to face her. "I'm going to assume that you've had too much to drink tonight," he said angrily. "You need to go home before you create any more problems for me."

"Problems?" she said. "How have I created any kind of problem? He had no idea what my questions were about. I promise you, I made them sound super casual."

"That's not the point," Charles said. "Say goodbye to everyone. I'm driving you home."

With that, Charles spun on his feet and headed back toward the party. Avery watched as his silhouette grew smaller the further away he got. Then, she let out a quiet and frustrated growl. It was loud enough to cause the ducks to erupt into chaos again.

Doesn't he know I'm just trying to help?

She wondered if she and Charles could ever be friends again. Everything she said and did seemed to upset him. She liked it better when he wasn't involved with the police force.

Then, he seemed to just let her be and do whatever she wanted.

By the time she made it back to the party to say her goodbyes, Charles was waiting impatiently for her in the car. Somewhat out of spite, she took her time.

It didn't bother her that she was leaving. The party was coming to an end, and most of the attendees had had too much to drink. People were hanging on each other, and a few tears were being cried. It was only a matter of time before someone would wind up dancing on the tables. Avery noticed the mayor seemed to be avoiding any real conversation with anyone.

Avery stood in the parking lot, wondering which direction she needed to walk to find Charles' car. It didn't take her long to find him, though. He was flashing his headlights at her impatiently.

"Took you long enough," Charles said as she climbed in.

"You said to say goodbye to *everybody*. So I did."

Charles clenched his jaw as he turned the key in the ignition. "We need to talk," he said gruffly.

Avery was having none of it. She was tired, her social battery was low, and she didn't like how Charles was behaving toward her. She wanted things to go back to normal. But, instead of saying that, she chose sarcasm. "What would you like to talk about?" she sang. "I'm so excited to share yet another cheerful conversation with you."

Chapter Eleven

The streets were quieter than they had been for weeks as Charles drove her home. With the festival over, most of the tourists had left, and the town was finally the quiet place Avery had grown to love.

Charles drove slowly, and it was agonizing. Avery didn't want to spend too much time in the car with him. She wanted to go home, sleep, and talk to him when she'd had enough time to think all possible conversations through. It felt like it was gearing up to be a conversation she needed to prepare for.

Still, she was stuck in the car with him. She had learned early on that it was best to get difficult conversations over with. It had saved her many days of sour feelings before, and she figured now would be the best time to talk.

"Forgive me if I'm more than a little frustrated with you," Charles said. "I'm sure I'm well within my right to be, considering you're doing everything in your power to screw this case up."

"Screw it up?" Avery said, shocked. "I'm trying to help. You don't need to be so stressed out all the time."

Charles had been correct when he implied that she'd had too much to drink. She was tipsy but far from drunk. She had just enough alcohol in her system, though, to remove any filter she once had over her words. Liquid courage is a dangerous thing.

Charles was about to say something when Avery saw the flesh beneath his eyes settle. He was beyond the point of being angry. He was tired of her. It didn't make her feel good.

"You're being completely reckless," he said helplessly. "All of what you're doing could be dangerous. Not only to the case but to you."

His knuckles were white from gripping the steering wheel, and she knew he was working hard at not completely losing his temper with her. At that moment, she pictured what he must have been like when he was a police officer.

"I can take care of myself," Avery said, turning to look out the window.

"That's not the point," Charles responded. "The point is that you keep sticking your nose where it doesn't belong. Not only do the police feel it is none of your business, but I'm also pretty sure the murderer feels that way too."

"The murderer?" she scoffed. "We don't even know who that is!"

"That's precisely the point," he pressed. "It could be any of a number of suspects. If the murderer realizes you know too much or feels like you're prying, you could be the next victim."

His words scared Avery enough to silence her.

"Besides," Charles continued. "There is no *we*. This is for the police department to handle, and you're not a police officer."

"Neither are you," she said under her breath.

"You're right." By that point, Charles sounded

completely exasperated with Avery. "But I am your friend, and I know a little about how these things work. I'm begging you, please leave it alone and let the police do their jobs."

They were quiet just as the car passed the mayor's house. Avery wondered if he was still enjoying the party or if her conversation with him had ruined his mood entirely. Perhaps he was having a drink to forget about the woman with the heron tattoo or even his conversation with Avery earlier. It hadn't occurred to her that she could be getting herself in trouble. She understood that she could be stubborn, but she was learning that she was easily the most stubborn person she knew.

"I'm sorry," she eventually said. "I just want to help."

"Please tell me you didn't talk to anyone else about it," Charles said. "The last thing we want is for the murderer to get spooked and leave town. The victim deserves for this case to be solved."

When he said it like that, she felt truly terrible. Still, she didn't like how Charles was speaking to her. It felt like she was in trouble with one of her parents, and she certainly didn't see Charles as a parental figure.

"So," he continued. "Would you please tell me about the conversation between you and the mayor? On the off-chance that there is something useful in there."

Avery sighed. "It wasn't much. He said his favorite bird was a heron, which I find interesting. Then he said he didn't attend the first day of the festival, which is weird. He also said he never knew the dead guy or the dead guy's wife."

"I don't even want to know how you managed to work all of that into one conversation and make it seem natural," Charles started. "It's just—never mind. Why do you say it's weird that he didn't attend the first day? Maybe he just had other plans."

"Because I saw him there, I'm sure of it," she explained. "He was sort of keeping to one side, but I am certain that it was him. He's the only person I know who wears glasses like that. He's the mayor; he's not that hard to recognize."

Charles hummed thoughtfully, "Hmmm."

"See? I think that's a little weird, don't you?"

"Well, if you saw him, then others surely saw him," Charles said. "And if he says he wasn't there, then perhaps he has an alibi, and you saw someone else."

"Yeah, but other people don't know what I know, so they'll think nothing of the fact that he was there that day. Or that he lies about having been there that day. I also learned that the postman had been complaining about a rude tourist, so I think there's a motive there," Avery rambled. "Also, how hard is it to fake an alibi? Most of us have friends who are willing to cover for us."

Charles glanced at Avery with a knowing look, and she sank back into her chair. She felt like a teenager who'd been caught drinking at a friend's house or something. It was bizarre. She was an adult, and still, she was in trouble.

"I wasn't doing anything illegal by talking to him," she defended herself.

Charles decided to ignore that statement completely.

"Do you remember what time you saw him?" Charles asked, taking more interest in it than Avery expected.

"I couldn't say, but it was somewhere between the grape-stomping competition and the concert."

The car fell silent again as they approached Avery's driveway. As usual, Sprinkles was outside waiting for her. Avery got out of the car, feeling completely defeated by the events of the day.

"Thanks for the ride home," she said, keeping her eyes on the ground.

"I thought you should know that Daya will likely be released," he said before she could close the door.

"Who's that?"

"The victim's wife," Charles said as if her name had been common knowledge. "We've questioned her, and she's not saying much. Without any concrete evidence, we'll have to let her go within the next twelve hours."

"Ah," she answered, raising her eyebrows. "Well, good luck."

Avery closed the door and left Charles in the driveway. She wasn't certain how she felt anymore. But she knew that the emotion was somewhere between disappointment and frustration. Coupled with that, she felt a small amount of guilt.

As Avery washed the smell of smoke off her body, she contemplated every word of her conversation with the mayor. Perhaps there was something he said that could be used to keep Daya detained for just a little while longer.

She wondered if it would have been different if she had waited to talk to Charles before following the woman to the mayor's house. She wondered why the mayor hadn't also been detained. She assumed it was because there was no proof that he had any knowledge of Daya's husband, to begin with.

If that were true, it would have been a much bigger shock to him than Avery had realized. And her bizarre choice of conversation would have been an awful reminder of his reality. Perhaps the mayor had been betrayed by her, just like she'd betrayed her husband.

Then she thought about the mayor at home again. Only, this time she wondered if he was completely heartbroken. She remembered the bags under his eyes and how late he was to the barbecue. Then, she pictured having to behave as professionally and cheerfully as he had, despite having just found out his lover was potentially a murderer.

"Oh, geez," she whispered as she covered her eyes with her palm. *How could I be so distasteful?*

It was, of course, easier to see it that way now that she had sobered up a little. She also understood Charles' behavior. Avery had spent too much time thinking of the suspects and hardly any time thinking of the victim.

She dragged herself out of the shower and put on dry clothes. Then, she sat down to craft a message to Charles. It took her some time because she didn't quite know how to put into words what she was feeling.

> *I'm sorry. I should have been more respectful. I should have checked with you first.*

She deleted it. She didn't like the tone, and it sounded too impersonal.

> *Charles, you've always been a good friend to me. I'm so sorry if I've crossed the line. I promise it won't happen again.*

She hit the delete key again. She couldn't make that promise. She was learning how stubborn she could be and couldn't be sure something like that wouldn't happen again.

> *It was irresponsible of me to do what I did; you're right. I was only trying to help in the way that I knew how. I never stopped to consider that perhaps nobody needed my help. I can't fix it, but I can promise to do better. I do hope that the police find the evidence they need to keep Daya detained. Keep me posted.*

She hit send. Avery figured it was the best that she had to offer. Still, she wasn't sure it would do the trick. She would simply have to wait until she saw Charles again to know exactly where they stood. She waited for his response. But it never came. And she couldn't sleep because of it. She didn't know if he had seen her message and read it and was ignoring her. Perhaps he was asleep. She wondered if he was at the police station, reporting back to them on the conversation she'd had with the mayor.

She had no way of knowing and it was driving her completely nuts.

Chapter Twelve

As usual, Avery's thoughts had kept her awake all night, and she had even darker bags beneath her eyes. She hadn't even bothered trying to cover them up with makeup. It had reached a point where they were so bad, makeup would have only made things worse.

When the doorbell rang, she was grateful to see her father's smiling face greet her. He would be the perfect distraction for her.

"How about some coffee, then?" her father asked. "It sure looks like you need it."

"Thanks, Dad," Avery said sarcastically. "Don't judge the bags under my eyes before you've seen your own."

"Pffft." Her dad waved away her remark. "Those are nothing. They've gotten way better since the doc gave me those sleeping tablets. Do you want some?"

"No, thank you, Dad," Avery laughed. "I think I'll need to have my brain removed before I'll be able to get a decent night's rest."

"Something on your mind?"

It was a beautiful winter's day in the vineyard, and the

guest house was quiet. For the most part, everything was under control. So, Avery and her dad headed out to walk in the vineyards as they sipped their coffee.

"You've really done a great job of getting the farm back on its feet," her father said. "I've always said you belong here. Not in the city."

"I miss the city sometimes," Avery said. "There, the drama all seemed far away from me. I mean, of course, there is worse crime and certainly more drama than here. But it seemed as if none of it affected me at all. It was just nothing more than stories in the news."

"Drama?" her father asked. "Has something happened?"

"Forget it," she said.

There was no way she could catch him up on everything that had happened over the previous few days. It was too much and too complicated. It would only make her parents worry. That was added stress that she couldn't afford. So, they walked in silence some more, but it didn't last very long.

"You never did tell me what's been bothering you so much that it keeps you awake," her father said.

Avery rolled her eyes. Her father never forgot anything. Even in his old age, it seemed his memory had only gotten better. Which only meant that as an adult, she got away with far less than she did as a child. At least back then, he had other things to occupy him, so most of what she did went unnoticed.

As an adult, with her parents living on the other end of the property, she couldn't get away with anything. He had nothing better to do, so he noticed everything.

She knew that she couldn't tell him everything. She had promised Charles she wouldn't, and if her father told her mother, which was likely, then it wouldn't be long before the entire town knew about it. Avery needed the perfect subject matter to steer the conversation away from what was on her mind.

"Hey, before I forget," she said cheerfully. "I met the mayor last night."

"Ah, yes," her father said with a smile. "Mayor Oswald. I know him quite well."

Avery looked at her father in shock. "You do?"

"Yes. We've both lived in this area equally as long. He and I met in the library many years ago. Well before he was the mayor here."

She couldn't imagine what it must have been like to live in such a small town before the invention of the Internet or television. Even now, there was little to do, and Avery relied perhaps a little too much on technology to keep her entertained.

She'd never met anybody in a library. In fact, even her books were online. It had been many years since she had last set foot in the library.

"Well, we didn't get to talk much. All I learned is that his favorite bird is a heron," she said.

She hadn't considered that the best way to get more information about the mayor might have been to ask somebody who knew him. It was even more perfect that the person was her father because he was less likely to find her line of questioning strange.

"A heron?" he asked. "That seems interesting."

"Interesting?" Avery laughed.

"It's just an odd choice," her father said, unknowingly agreeing with her. "Most people's favorite birds are parrots or flamingos or something like that, you know. I've never heard of anybody's favorite bird being a heron."

"Well, maybe it reminds him of his wife or something," Avery said, hoping to find out more about the mayor's past life.

"Oh no, Oswald's never been married," her father explained. "It seems a pity since he is so likable. He's the only mayor I know that insists people refer to him by his first name."

"His first name is Oswald?" Avery asked in shock.

"Oh yes," her father laughed. "Did you not know that? It's a family name. His surname is Peters."

"Now that seems backward," Avery chuckled. "So he was really never married?"

"No, he focused on his career his entire life. As far as I know, he lost his parents when he was quite young. He's really only ever relied on himself. Which makes his achievements all the more impressive," her father explained. "I don't know what I would have done without your mother by my side."

"That's how I felt about James," Avery commented. "And yet, here I am."

She motioned to the vines around her. She couldn't help but relate to the dried out branches that she saw ahead of her. The stems seemed just as twisted and heavy as her thoughts. Although the parts of the vine that lay above the surface were all but dead, what happened below was nothing short of remarkable.

The most important person in her life had died, leaving her as nothing more than a shell of the woman that she had been. And yet, every other part of her had seemed to fall into place.

"Here you are," her father said with a sympathetic smile.

"So how do you think he did it?" she asked. "How do you think he made it through everything alone?"

"It's that military training, I tell you," her father answered.

"He served? He doesn't seem the type." Avery thought back to the man she had spoken to at the side of the pond.

He had seemed so soft and quiet. She was having a hard time imagining him in his uniform, wielding a weapon.

"The man he is today is nothing like the man he once was," her father explained. "I've seen the medals in his house. That man has done more than most to protect this country. Besides, from what I hear, he's a really good man. Every month he goes over to the postman's house to help him in the garden. He's the only friend the postman really has."

"How does one go from serving in the military to being the mayor in a town like this one?" she eventually asked.

The ground was damp beneath her feet as they walked side by side. The steam from their coffee cups wafted clouds in front of them, and every time she took a sip, the warmth would burn the tip of her cold nose.

"Well, it wasn't quite as easy as you make it sound," her father chuckled. "When he could no longer stand fighting in the war, he decided to do something to more directly protect the people. He joined the police force."

"Mayor Oswald Peters was a police officer?" Avery asked, stunned.

"I'm not sure why this surprises you so much," her father shrugged. "Many police officers find themselves going into politics."

Avery wondered what it meant for the case. It was probable that more than a few people had worked on the force with the mayor at some point. It would make it incredibly difficult to look into him properly as a suspect. And his close friendship with the postman made it impossible to look into the postman as a suspect too. It certainly explained why Charles seemed so convinced that the mayor was a victim.

"So, how did he wind up here exactly?" she asked.

"He was serving on a force in a larger city. He had even been offered a promotion to detective. But then, one day, he got called out to a pretty rough scene. Something changed in him, and he simply couldn't face it anymore."

Her father paused to take a long sip of his coffee, peering into the bottom of his cup when the sip wasn't quite as big as he'd hoped. Avery turned them back toward the house. Her cup was also nearly empty, and she was certain she would need another.

"He declined the offer for promotion," her father continued. "He asked to be transferred somewhere with a lower crime rate, hoping for a quieter life."

"I see," Avery said softly. "I didn't know any of this about him."

"I didn't know that his favorite bird is a heron," her father said. "So why are you so interested in our mayor anyway?"

Her father raised an eyebrow at her like he often had when he was insinuating that perhaps there was more than met the eye.

"I'm just trying to make some more friends," Avery said before rolling her eyes. "Besides, I didn't even tell you the best part."

"Oh?"

"He says that the Le Blanc Cellars Chenin Blanc is his favorite," Avery said with a proud smile.

Her father smiled, too. He tapped one of the vines as if to congratulate it on producing a wine fine enough to be the mayor's favorite. "Then we should name the wine after him," her father said.

Avery laughed. "That seems a little drastic," Avery said. "Besides, you never know if he was just simply trying to be polite."

"Then perhaps I should give you his address. Send him a case of it," her father suggested.

It wasn't a terrible idea, but Avery shuddered to think

exactly how upset Charles would be if she did that. It would be completely inappropriate, given the circumstances. She could just hear him telling her that she was once again crossing the line.

"Better yet," her father continued. "Why don't I set up a time to have coffee with him? I've been meaning to catch up with him for quite some time. You can come with me, and we can give him the bottles personally."

"Oh, no, thank you, Dad," she said. "I think I'll pass on that one. But if you do see him, please give him my regards."

As soon as they stepped back into the warmth of her home, she poured them both another cup of coffee. They sat at the kitchen table as they often had when she was younger and sipped their coffee in silence.

She was grateful for her father's visit. Not only for the pleasant distraction from her own thoughts. But he had told her so much about the mayor that she hadn't known before. But none of it had answered any of her questions. Why had he lied about being at the first day of the festival? And why did he not mention that he knew the wife of the victim?

"You know, your mother has been talking to the women of the book club," her father said suddenly. "She says the one woman has a niece whose good friend is currently shacked up with a police officer. She told your mother that the dead man from the festival had been found with large stacks of cash in his shoes."

Avery stared at her father with a knowing look.

"I didn't believe it either," he laughed. "But I thought it was interesting to see exactly how far the rumors had already traveled. I won't be surprised if soon there's someone claiming that he's half-robot."

If only he knew that she held the most precious infor-mation of all regarding the case. On her phone, she had photographs of the town's beloved and decorated mayor kissing the wife of the dead victim. And she would never tell a soul.

"I just hope they find the culprit soon," her father continued. "The whole thing has your mother very stressed out. You know how she is when people die."

Avery nodded. "I remember after that time when one of the chickens met an unsavory end. She nearly got an armed guard up in front of the coop!"

Her mother had a way of taking even the smallest situation and making it into a very big deal. She remembered it all too well and shuddered to think what her mother would make if she knew the truth about the dead man.

Her father nodded and laughed. "Precisely! Now we've got a man dead at the wine festival, and your mother is too afraid to have a second glass with dinner in case she drinks herself to death!"

If only her mother knew that the man had been poisoned. Avery wondered if perhaps then her mother would refuse to drink anything at all.

Chapter Thirteen

By the time her father left, Avery was eager for some quiet time alone. She'd been happy about his visit, but he had a habit of staying just a few minutes too long and talking just a little too slowly. At first, she thought the visit with her father would clear her mind of the repeated thoughts about the dead man and his cheating wife. Instead, she had only learned more about the mayor, which steered her thoughts in a completely different direction—direction she wished she had never been steered in. *What if he's in danger? What if she intends to do it again? It could be an insurance scam...I'm sure the mayor has excellent life insurance.*

Her thoughts were running entirely out of control, and she needed a way to reel them back in. At times, when her thoughts ran away from her like that, she understood why her mother sometimes went overboard in response to bad news. Perhaps her mother was acting out on her own chaotic thoughts.

It was clear that Oswald was a man who had dedicated

his life to the service of others. It is a rare quality to find in a person. She wondered how much he knew about the case. Given that he had been in the police force before and was the mayor, it was likely that he'd been given a fair amount of information. But he also happened to be in a relationship with the victim's wife. So, perhaps they hadn't told him all that much information because of that.

Avery tidied up the coffee cups and wondered what she would do for the rest of the cold wintery day. She needed to do something to keep herself busy. One part of her brain was telling her to get to the mayor and warn him about the potential danger that he was in. Nobody wants to know that they are in a relationship with a murderer. But still, it is better to know than not to know.

He's a military man and a police officer. He can take care of himself, certainly better than you can protect him. You're just being silly. Calm down. That thought temporarily put her mind at ease. She hopped in the shower and got ready for the day. Still, when she was clean and fresh, she had nothing to do for the day.

Then, another thought undid her mind once more. *He's in love. He will be blind to it all. We've all made stupid choices in the name of love. And he is only human, after all.*

She'd had enough of her own thoughts and panic. She was stressed about a man that she barely knew. A man that she had promised Charles she would not speak to again regarding anything to do with Daya.

She needed a better distraction. So, after a quick few messages, it was arranged that the women of the Stammtisch would be getting together at her house for lunch. But that was still hours away.

Avery made the cold walk over to the wine room. It was decorated for winter, with small crystals hanging from the rafters. She quite enjoyed the effect that it had, casting little rainbows throughout the room every time the light streamed in.

She only caught a glimpse of Charles. As she walked in, he had darted off toward the storeroom. She hated going into the storeroom. She had no idea what was going on in there; everything was piled up so high, and it felt like a tiny maze inside. It made her too stressed out. Most of the time, she left the storeroom up to Charles to manage. She trusted him enough to do so.

Avery waited at the counter for Charles to return. But he took longer than usual. When he returned, she thought it was odd that he had taken so long. His arms were empty, so he wasn't fetching anything from the room. Why had he been in there so long?

"Morning, Charles," she said cheerfully.

She received nothing but silence from him as he put the few bottles he had collected onto the shelves. Avery reached for the visitor's book to see how the customers had been doing lately. She was pleased to see that every entry was positive and that some customers had returned multiple times.

"This looks great! Are you enjoying the tastings?" she asked, looking up at Charles.

Again, he said absolutely nothing and walked back toward the storeroom to disappear for another few minutes. She wasn't sure it was appropriate for him to behave that way, given that she was his boss. The last person she had expected the silent treatment from would be Charles. He was clearly more upset with her than she had initially realized. She didn't quite understand why he was all that upset. She knew she had crossed a line, but they'd already had an argument over it. Why would he just stop talking to her?

She didn't have the time to sit and figure it out, either.

She needed to prepare for lunch with the Stammtisch women. She slid her chair out and left it that way, knowing that it was an easy way to irk Charles. *Two can play this game.*

Her home was cheerful when the Stammtisch women arrived. Avery had set out fresh flowers and her best glasses and dinnerware. The shrimp étouffée she had prepared for the ladies was just about ready, and Avery couldn't wait to feed her friends. She was in the mood to enjoy her day for the first time in a week. The women seemed to be matching her energy too.

Within minutes, her home was full of chatter and cheerful conversation, and Avery was able to forget all about the dead man, his wife, the mayor, and Charles' odd behavior.

That is until lunch was done, and it was time to clear the table. Tiffany had stayed behind to help, despite Avery's insistence that she preferred to do it alone.

"What's been up with you lately?" Tiffany asked as they dried the dishes.

"What do you mean?"

"You seem upset. I understand everything with the heron tattooed woman, but I've known you for long enough to know that something else is bothering you."

There was only one person that Avery trusted other than Charles, and that was Tiffany. Avery sighed as she took a seat at the table, motioning for Tiffany to join her.

"I spoke to the mayor the other night at the barbecue," she said. "He said he didn't know the dead guy or Daya."

"Daya?"

"The dead guy's wife," Avery explained. "He said he wasn't there on the first day of the festival, and it made me confused. But then I learned from my dad that he was in the military and the police force. Now, I think he might just be involved with a dangerous woman and not even know about it."

Tiffany stared at Avery for a while. "Okay, yes, I understand why that is upsetting. But how did you get to talking to him about the dead guy in the first place? You don't even know the man."

"I don't know. I just worked it into the conversation somehow," Avery said. "Anyway, Charles is so upset with me that he won't even talk to me anymore."

"That seems like a little overkill," Tiffany said. "But if you need me to talk to him for you, I will."

Avery chuckled. "No, that's alright. I'm a big girl. I can sort this out on my own."

Tiffany seemed pleased with those answers. The two of them finished cleaning up, and she was on her way. Avery was about to get into bed when her phone rang. It was Deb. It was an odd time of night to be calling, but Avery figured she must have just left something behind.

"Hi, Deb," Avery answered. "Did you forget something?"

"No," Deb answered. "I just heard about Charles. Why didn't you say anything?"

For a moment, Avery wondered if Tiffany had already told her about their conversation but knew that it was unlikely. Tiffany had never been much of a gossip.

"I don't understand," Avery said. "What about Charles?"

"Don't you know?" Deb sounded shocked. "I have a friend who has a friend who has been dating one of our police officers. She says that Charles was in trouble with the mayor. Says that he had taken photos of the mayor in a compromising position without any authority to do so."

Avery's stomach dropped. "No, I hadn't heard about that."

"Anyway," Deb continued undisrupted. "Turns out he was let off early, but he can no longer be involved with the police force in any way."

She couldn't stand the thought of it. Charles had taken the fall for her. He had sacrificed something of great importance to him in order to keep her out of trouble. That would certainly explain the way he was behaving. "Are you sure?" Avery asked, nervous about the answer.

"Yes," Deb said. "I think it has something to do with one of their high-profile cases. Why else would Charles be doing such strange things?"

He wouldn't. Avery knew that, and so did Charles, and so did Tiffany. But she had no idea how to put it into words.

"Apparently, he faced quite serious charges, but because of his previous service to the town, the mayor agreed to drop them all if he simply resigned as a consultant to the police force," Deb finished.

Now she understood. She couldn't say anything, and Charles took the fall for her because the charges against her would have been far more severe. Charles had a certain level of protection that Avery would not have been afforded.

"Thanks for letting me know, Deb," Avery said, feeling completely defeated.

"No problem!" Deb sang. "Still, I think we should do something nice for him, you know, to cheer him up. I know how important it all was to him."

Avery ended the call and got out of bed. There was no way she would be able to fall asleep easily that night. She no longer cared at all about the safety of the mayor. She cared only about Charles and how he would be feeling. He had taken a large knock because of her reckless behavior. She absolutely hated the thought of it. She reached for her phone and once again typed out message after message to him, each of which was quickly deleted.

A message simply wouldn't suffice. She needed to make it right, but she needed time to figure out how. At that moment, she feared that she had lost Charles as a friend, and it broke her heart completely.

Chapter Fourteen

When the sun filtered its light through her curtains, Avery knew the best way to make things right with Charles would be to talk to him. He would know what she could do. But in order to talk to him about it, she needed him to talk to her first.

It was no secret that he wasn't on talking terms with her. Nobody had treated her like that in years, and it was working on her nerves. But she couldn't blame him for it, either.

Avery's plan to make that happen was to make sure he couldn't possibly avoid her. And in order to do that, she was going to annoy him into paying attention to her. She had already planned it all out.

Avery snuck into the wine room before Charles showed up for his shift, and made her way through the maze of wine boxes in the storeroom. She took deep breaths to avoid claustrophobia and made herself as small as possible behind some boxes. Then, she waited. It should only have been a few minutes before Charles arrived at work. But as luck would have it, he was late that day.

Despite the boredom of waiting for someone between those boxes, Avery hadn't gone to the bathroom before she hid. So, her eagerness for him to arrive at work was becoming urgent.

She heard the sound of the door being unlocked and opened. Then, she heard him walk over to the keypad to deactivate the alarm. Of course, the alarm would already have been deactivated. Avery chuckled as she heard him mutter under his breath about it. He had never forgotten to activate the alarm.

"Hello?" Charles called through the wine room.

But Avery kept quiet. Her plan was to wait until he came to get the first box of stock, which was routine for Charles to do as soon as he had wiped the counters. Then, Avery would jump out and surprise him. She was certain that he would get a big fright and that it would force him to say at least one word to her, even if it was a curse word. But only as she was already tucked away, silent, and hidden, did it occur to her that he might mistake her for an intruder.

It wasn't going to work, but it was too late to change her plan. She was already there, and Charles would be coming into the storeroom at any moment. She needed to abort the mission somehow. She clearly hadn't thought it through well enough.

Avery got out from her hiding spot and called back to him. "It's me; I'm in here, just looking for something!" She waited to hear if he would respond. But he only let out a little unamused huff and carried on about his business.

Avery needed a different plan. Something that would get his attention without making him afraid or possibly give him a reason to feel that he needed to defend himself.

She popped her head around the corner. "Charles," she called out. "Where do we keep those few boxes of the special red blend?" She knew where they were; she just needed him to say something. "There's no need to stop what you're doing. You can just direct me toward them," she said. *Chicken. Why don't you just tell him you know what happened? There is no need for you to go about it this way at all.* "I can't seem to find it, and I've been searching for some time," she said anyway.

Charles looked up at her with a completely blank stare. He left the wine-tasting counter and made his way toward her. He didn't even need to enter the storeroom. He simply pointed at the stack of boxes right next to the door and left silently again.

Avery could feel her cheeks getting warm with embarrassment. Of course, they would be right next to the door. She should have checked before she continued on with that plan. "Ah," she said sheepishly. "Of course, that was the last place I would have looked."

Just as she thought she had enough confidence to approach the topic of discussion with him, a group of tourists walked in for a wine tasting. She would have to wait.

Charles was a smart man, and he knew that she was waiting for him. So, he took his time with the tourists, giving them what was likely the best wine tasting of their lives. Avery was pleased, despite the amount of time it took, as the tourists left with a large stack of boxes, each filled with six bottles of wine.

When it had finally quieted down again, she took a seat at the counter. Charles was about to leave, but she wouldn't let him. "I know what happened," she said quietly.

Avery saw his shoulders drop as he let out a loud sigh. Still, he remained quiet. She had thought of so many different ways to apologize to him, but at that moment, she had hit a complete blank. "You didn't have to do that. I can take responsibility for what I did," she said.

"It's not that simple," Charles mumbled. "He was ready to take some serious action."

"That's okay. It was my fault, my responsibility," she pressed.

Charles spun around. "Don't you get it?" he snapped. "You could have faced jail time. If I took the blame, I would get no jail time. I still have my job here, so the repercussions were far less severe."

"I'm sorry," she said, knowing that the words alone would never be enough. "I don't know what else to say."

"Why don't you just promise me you'll butt out?" he asked. "I asked you so many times to let it go, and you didn't listen. It was reckless, Avery."

"I know," she complained. "I wish I could take it back, but I can't. I guess I didn't think it would come to this."

"I tried to warn you that it would. If you would just have listened to me!"

She felt terrible. The entire time she had felt as if Charles hadn't been listening to her or taking her seriously. Instead, the truth had been the opposite. She wasn't taking him seriously, and he was the one who paid the price for it.

"I thought the photographs were sent in anonymously," she said.

"Yeah, well, turns out the mayor has some ties in the police force," he mumbled. "And the anonymous tip was still sent from my cell phone."

She had forgotten about that part. He had done it for her. The whole thing was a mess. She had been so worried about what kind of danger the mayor had been in, despite the fact that he was a stranger to her, she had never considered the risk that Charles had taken every time he had helped her.

"It's true. He worked as a police officer for quite some time," Avery said. "I asked my dad about it."

"So you still didn't drop it?" he asked. "After you told me that you would?"

Avery looked down at her hands. "It wasn't like that at all. I was just telling my dad that I had met the mayor, and he told me they were friends. He told me some information about him. I wasn't looking for it, I promise!"

His one eyebrow rose, causing a wrinkle to form across his forehead and Avery knew that he simply didn't believe her. And he didn't have a reason to believe her, either. She had promised him twice that she wouldn't get involved, and each time she had broken that promise.

"I'm sorry," she said again.

"Never mind," Charles said as if Avery still didn't get it. He turned around and carried on with his task at hand. "It doesn't matter now anyway. Just be careful because I cannot help you again. I can't have anything to do with the police."

"It matters to me," she said.

"Is that why you've been hanging out here for hours?" he asked. "How did you hear about it anyway?"

"Deb called last night. She knows someone who knows somebody," she said quietly. "How did the mayor find out about the photographs?"

"They had shown it to Daya during her interrogation. She must have told him about it," he answered. "You can imagine a man like him would do whatever it takes to keep something like that from spreading."

There was a silence between them. "Just promise me you haven't said anything to anyone about the photographs. Because if you did, then I could be in even greater trouble."

Avery swallowed hard. "No, I haven't told anyone. Tiffany knows because she was with me, but she's agreed not to tell a soul."

"Right," he said. "Well, if that's all, then I am going to

take my coffee break. It is eleven o'clock now, and I'm desperate for a pick-me-up."

"Eleven?" Avery asked as she dropped the book that was in front of her. "Shoot, I gotta go."

She had completely forgotten that she'd planned to take Sprinkles to obedience training. She had found a course online that was not too far from her, but it started at eleven-thirty and was at least a twenty-five minute-drive away.

First, she had to find Sprinkles. Avery raced through the property, calling for her dog. She didn't even care how many guests she bothered in the process; she needed to hurry up. She had his leash and collar tucked into her back pocket when she found the dog rolling around in a patch of dirt.

"Come, Sprinkles!" she called. "We need to hurry up."

Thankfully for Avery, Sprinkles loved nothing more than to go for a drive. So, the moment she opened the car door, the dog jumped right inside. "Good boy," she said as she raced around to the other side. "Time to get you trained so you can be the good dog you were destined to be."

For the entire drive to the training grounds, she replayed the conversation with Charles in her head. She had never seen him look so down and heartbroken, and she wished she knew what to do about it. She thought about all the ways she could potentially make it up to him.

Avery couldn't understand why he would have gone so out of his way to protect her. She was his boss, and most people would be thrilled to be rid of their bosses. Surely he didn't love his job at the vineyard more than he loved consulting for the police?

Chapter Fifteen

The scene between Brie, the dog trainer, and Sprinkles was like something out of a movie. The trainer behaved as if she was training Sprinkles to go to war. For a short while, it did look a little like a war, with Sprinkles running aimlessly through the field as the trainer tried desperately to get the situation under control.

It had started to look to Avery as if there was little hope that Sprinkles would ever be a well-behaved dog.

"Right now, Sprinkles!" Brie shouted. "Fall in line!"

Avery laughed. There was no way on Earth Sprinkles would understand that command. Still, Brie waited expectantly with her hair slicked back into a tight, neat bun. She even went as far as to consult the watch strapped to her wrist while impatiently tapping her foot against the ground.

By the time they were done, Sprinkles was so exhausted he fell onto his side and took a nap.

"Well, Sprinkles sure is energetic," Brie said with a chuckle.

"Yes," Avery agreed. "Which is why you are so necessary. Thank you."

"Don't worry. I'll get Sprinkles behaving in no time. I've dealt with worse," Brie responded as she wiped the sweat from her face.

"Do you get a lot of difficult students?" Avery asked.

"Not that much, but I was a trainer in the military for a long time. That's where I dealt with the truly difficult students."

Avery looked at Brie and could see it clearly. The slicked-back bun, the neat clothes, and the strict way in which she spoke to the dogs suddenly all made sense. It even looked as if her t-shirt had been crisply ironed, something Avery would never do.

"You were in the military?" Avery asked, trying not to sound too shocked. "How did you wind up being a dog trainer?"

"Well, I trained dogs in the military," Brie responded. "I guess after a while, I wanted to put my work into something that felt a little more rewarding. I lost a lot of students, and it became difficult for me."

"I'm sorry to hear that," Avery said shyly. "How long were you in the military?"

"I served for around ten years, training strictly military dogs. That's where I met most of the people I know today. I even trained the dog that saved our mayor's life!"

Brie smiled widely at her, and Avery couldn't believe how small the world could truly be. Brie seemed friendly and eager to talk. So, Avery decided that she would see how much information she could get on their mayor while she still had the chance.

"You served with the mayor?" she said, surprised. "I only met him for the first time the other day."

"I did." Brie nodded and looked into the distance as if she was searching the field for a distant memory. It seemed a little dramatic to Avery.

"He was an excellent man. He's the reason I decided to keep training dogs. I was willing to give it up entirely!" Brie said.

"If you don't mind me asking...what happened?"

Brie and Avery made themselves comfortable on a nearby bench as Sprinkles lay fast asleep at Avery's feet.

"Well, after I left the military, I had lost so many dogs that I found it difficult to spend any time with them. The dogs, that is," Brie explained. "I had spoken to Oswald about it. Told him that even though I knew what the dogs were doing was important, I cared about them too much."

"That's understandable," Avery interjected.

"Yeah, and he understood it perfectly," Brie continued. "And then I went on to explain to him that I had become so afraid of getting attached to the dogs that even outside of the military, I didn't think I could continue to train them."

Brie took a sip of her water and sighed. "The problem is that the dogs will never outlive us, which bothers me tremendously. Those dogs were sent to be a part of a war they had nothing to do with. I felt incredible guilt for it."

Avery could see the struggle in Brie's eyes as she spoke about it. It was apparent that traces of that guilt were still there. Brie had been perfectly poised the entire time she had conducted the training. But as she spoke about her experience, she suddenly became fidgety. Her fingers trembled as they tugged at anything they could find.

"Well, I couldn't get myself to look at any dog without feeling immense guilt for what I had been a part of," she continued. "I really have loved every single dog I have ever worked with...Sprinkles being next on the list."

Brie looked down at Sprinkles and smiled. "I felt I had done the dogs a great disservice for what I had been preparing them for. And after I left the military, the only job

I was offered was to train dogs for the police force, which felt like basically the same thing."

Avery glanced at Sprinkles and tried to imagine him trying to do the work as a police dog or a dog on a battle-field. The mental image was something similar to a circus.

"But when Oswald heard that I had given up my career of dog training, he showed up at my house unannounced with his dog, Smith," Brie said with a smile. "He insisted that I train his dog and refused to let anybody else do it."

"Does everyone, including the dog in that family, have last names for first names?" Avery laughed.

"It would appear so!" Brie chuckled. "Well, I didn't want to do it at first. And in reality, I was upset that he'd even suggested it. But he was so stubborn and insistent that I eventually agreed but swore it would be the last dog I ever trained."

"Is he really that stubborn?" Avery asked, eager to learn more about the man.

"One of the most stubborn men I know," Brie commented. "Anyway, when I trained his dog, I realized quickly that training people's pets is a far more rewarding experience than I had anticipated. The chances of them living long lives and growing old are high. It made me realize I could continue to do this." Brie motioned at the field in front of her. Avery could only assume she was referring to the fact that it was where she did the training and wasn't referring to the actual ground itself. Avery did her best to hide a small smile.

She liked the idea that Mayor Oswald had such a caring nature. She wasn't a fan of anyone quite that stubborn, but she could appreciate his kindness. It had only mace her come to the conclusion that he couldn't have known his lover was the dead man's wife. Someone with that amount of kindness could never get involved with a married woman. Avery was certain of it.

"Well, Sprinkles and I are so grateful that you have decided to continue your training," Avery said gently.

Brie packed up the rest of her belongings and gave Sprinkles a big kiss on his head before leaving Avery and Sprinkles in the park. Desperate for a quieter night, Avery decided to see how much more of Sprinkles' energy she could deplete by taking him for a brisk walk before heading home.

She had almost forgotten entirely about her conversation with Charles. The training and the dog trainer had been a brilliant distraction. It had even gotten her to laugh for the first time in a while. She wished that feeling could have carried on.

The closer she got to home, the more guilt crept in for her. She had cost Charles a lot. But she had also learned a lot about the mayor. His behavior regarding the photographs made more sense to her now.

He was a kind but stubborn man. It was more than likely that Daya had led him on and manipulated him. She hated the idea that Daya could potentially ruin the name of such a good man. And she could feel the anger growing inside her. But she could do nothing. She had already done enough harm. She needed to take a step back and keep her promise to Charles.

Sprinkles slept the entire drive home. And when they got home, he drank some water and went to his bed to sleep some more. It meant Avery could have the first restful sleep in a long time, until around five o'clock in the morning when an intrusive thought woke her from her peaceful sleep.

If he's so great, then why is he not married?

She understood not everyone wants to get married and

have that kind of life, but he really seemed to her like someone who would be interested in it. Thankfully, he was a public figure, so it wasn't very difficult for Avery to get her hands on the information.

"Mrs. Peters," she said with a satisfied grin as she scrolled the web page with all his information. There she could see the years in which he had served in the military and the police force. She could see some of the details of his campaign to be mayor. And she could see the information about his wife. He'd been married before he had moved to their town. It certainly explained why his father said he hadn't ever been married.

He had married a school teacher. And, if the photographs were anything to go by, they were perfectly happy. So where was she? The page didn't say, but Avery was certain she knew where to look.

It didn't take long for her to find the mayor's wife on social media. In a world so small, and due to the fact that everyone around her seemed to be friends with Mayor Oswald, she figured that there were likely some friends in common.

She had to scroll an absurdly far distance, but she eventually found what she had been looking for. She could read through Mrs. Peters' updates and gather that she and the mayor had separated at one point.

Part of Avery was relieved, knowing that the mayor wasn't having an affair against his wife also. But another part of her thoughts traveled down a new and frustrating path. *If he's so great, then why did they split?*

Chapter Sixteen

A very pondered the split between the mayor and his wife for most of the morning. It made her feel foolish, but she couldn't help herself. It wasn't any of her business, but it had changed the way she had originally felt about the mayor. So, it meant it was important.

She wished she could just ask one of them about it, but how could she possibly do that without it seeming as if she might be prying? She could invite the mayor over for some of his favorite Chenin Blanc and work it into the conversation. But she was certain that after their last conversation, he wouldn't be so keen.

Before she could finish that thought, a loud clattering sound came from the other end of the house. Avery ran toward the sound, bracing herself for what she might find. But all she found was Sprinkles, standing in the center of the dining room table.

A bird flew over Sprinkles' head as he tried to snatch it out of the air. Avery, not wanting to deal with the feathery mess that would be left behind should Sprinkles have succeeded, ran toward them to come to the bird's rescue.

She hadn't anticipated, though, that the bird was in no mood to be rescued. No matter how hard Avery tried to guide the bird in the right direction, it wouldn't get the hint. It swooped over her head, crashing into and knocking things over.

Eventually, the bird had come to its own defense, swooping down to hit Avery on the head as it passed. Avery rubbed her head and took a step back to assess all the ways she could've handled the situation a little better.

"I'm just going to leave you alone," she finally concluded.

She slumped down on the couch and caught her breath. As with any other moment when she wasn't immediately distracted, she thought about Charles and the mayor. She needed to decide what she was going to do.

Mayor Oswald was a good man who was in potential danger. Everybody seemed to love him and sing his praises, and she didn't want anything to happen to him, knowing that she might have been able to warn him and prevent it all.

Then again, she had known Charles for longer, and she had already done enough harm to him. She had made him a promise to stay out of it, and she felt obliged to keep that promise.

Whatever. He's already mad at me. The damage had already been done with Charles. How could she justify it if the mayor turned up murdered too?

Avery raced through a shower and got ready. She peered into the dining room to conclude that the bird was still creating a large mess, and Sprinkles was still making his best attempt at hunting. Then, knowing they'd both be busy for a while, she left.

She felt increasingly anxious as she raced toward the mayor's house. She was worried that she might already have been too late. *What if she's already murdered him? What if it's my fault for not saying something?* By the time she reached his driveway, she had been driving so fast that her brakes made a screeching sound as she came to a stop. Then, anxious and out of breath, Avery clambered out of her car and sped toward his front door.

She couldn't even ring the bell before the door swung open. The mayor looked completely shocked at her arrival at his front door, and she couldn't blame him.

"Avery, what can I do for you?" he said, trying desperately to keep his composure. He had remembered her name. He really was an excellent man.

"Mayor Oswald," Avery greeted, out of breath. "I'm so happy you're alright." The words had slipped out before she'd given herself a chance to contemplate them better. The mayor gave her a confused look.

"What do you mean?" he asked. He was no fool. He could see the concern on Avery's face. "Would you like a glass of water?" he asked. Avery nodded. Mayor Oswald welcomed her into his home and made her comfortable at the kitchen counter.

She took a look around. His home was neat, as she would expect from a military man. She took a moment to look at his décor and the images he chose to decorate his walls with and made a note that not a single item contained the image of a heron.

"So, what can I do for you?" he asked again, smiling kindly at her.

"I need to warn you about something," Avery said, taking a large sip of water.

"Oh?"

"It's kind of difficult to explain to you how or why I know, and what the full story is. But I really need you to listen to me," she said. Mayor Oswald leaned forward in his chair and focused entirely on her.

"It's about Daya," she eventually said, looking down at her hands.

"I see," the Mayor responded calmly. "What seems to be the problem?"

"I know why your favorite bird is a heron," Avery said, pointing to the back of her neck. "It's because of Daya."

Mayor Oswald clenched his jaw. "I was hoping it hadn't become common knowledge," he said.

"It hasn't," Avery said quickly. "I promise. As I said, it's complicated."

He stared blankly at her for a while then glanced her over as if to try and judge whether or not she was being truthful. "Alright, well, what is this about then?" the mayor continued.

"I suppose by now you know that she was married to the man who had died at the festival," Avery said, looking at him for a response.

"This explains your bizarre conversation with me the other night," the mayor responded. "You already knew."

Avery shrugged the comment off. She didn't want to admit to anything, and she didn't want to waste any more time. She could see that the mayor was getting concerned, and it was clear she was out of line. But he was patient with her, and she was there and had already said too much. She couldn't stop it now.

"Well, I think she is a dangerous woman," Avery said suddenly.

"You think she's guilty," he said quietly.

"I think it is highly possible," Avery said. "I found some stones on the festival grounds, and I think they were a clue."

"Stones?"

"When her husband was found dead, he had a stone in his hand that had the word Heron on it," she explained. "The only thing that troubles me is where she got the stones. It seems they came from the postman's garden pond? Did you ever take her with you to visit him?"

"Yes, she came with me once to help him in the garden."

The moment she said it, she saw something in his eyes change. She wasn't sure what it was, but it looked like fear. And she knew that she was getting through to him.

"Continue," he said sternly.

"Well, the next night, when I was helping clean the grounds. I found two more stones," she explained. "I took them to the police. They read *Follow* and *The*."

"Follow the heron," Mayor Oswald said as his face paled.

"Yes," Avery agreed. "I took them to the police, but they thought perhaps it had just been a coincidence. You know, some stones that were left behind."

"But you don't think so?" he asked.

"No," Avery said. "See, he bumped into me the night that he died. He was stumbling, and most of us just assumed he was drunk. But he kept repeating himself, and after I found the stones, his words really bothered me."

The mayor wasn't taking his eyes off her anymore, and she knew that he was truly listening to her. For the first time since it had all begun, someone was really listening and believing.

"What was he saying?" the mayor asked sternly.

"She did it," Avery said. "She's the one you're looking for."

The room fell silent, and Avery didn't know what to do. The mayor glanced down, deep in thought, clenching his jaw.

"As I said," Avery continued. "We all thought he just had too much to drink. Of course, now we know he was poisoned."

His head shot up as he looked at her. "How do you know that?"

Avery pinched her eyes closed. She couldn't get anyone in any more trouble. All that mattered was that the mayor remained safe.

"That doesn't matter," she said, brushing off the question. "What matters is that when I spotted the heron tattoo on the back of Daya's neck, it all fell into place for me."

"And what did you decide happened?"

It felt like an odd question, but Avery could understand that the mayor was likely in shock and definitely rather uncomfortable.

"I think she poisoned him," she said. "When I saw her at the coffee shop, she didn't look at all like a woman who had lost her husband. I know what that's like. She was smiling and laughing only days after it had happened."

The mayor sighed. He leaned back in his chair and tapped his hand on the table. He was upset, it was clear, and he had every right to be.

"My reasoning for having a heron as a favorite bird could have meant anything," the mayor said. "Your conversation with me at the barbecue and your conversation with me now leaves me with an important question."

"Yes?" Avery answered, wishing he wouldn't ask it.

"How do you know about Daya and me?"

She knew the question was coming, and she didn't want to answer it. But she would. And she would set things straight for Charles.

"I'm the one who took the photographs," she admitted, keeping her eyes downcast. "I agreed to keep it anonymous, and I never had the intention of telling anyone other than the police."

He remained silent.

"I assure you, I simply got carried away," she continued. "I am aware now of how inappropriate it was, and I promise you, I never intended to overstep such a large boundary."

"Charles took the fall for you," he said as he pieced it together. "And he stopped you at the barbecue, too."

"Yes," Avery said. "He didn't have to, but I guess he is a better friend to me than I had thought. I took it for granted."

"Does anybody else know about any of this?" he asked.

"No, well, I tried to speak to the police and Charles, but they don't believe me. I've been asked to butt out."

"And here you are," he said with a smile.

"Yes," she said sheepishly. "Here I am."

Chapter Seventeen

Avery wasn't sure whether to feel proud or ashamed for how she had intruded on the mayor's evening. She also couldn't quite read his body language as well as she would have liked. It was difficult to know if he was upset or otherwise. She had just dropped a bombshell on him and hadn't considered yet how he might react to the information.

"Thank you for coming to tell me," he said calmly, getting up to pour himself a cup of water. "I am sure it couldn't have been an easy decision to make."

Avery sighed a quiet sigh of relief. "I couldn't sleep. I had to let you know that you were potentially in danger. Please, just know that I won't tell anybody about any of this; you have my word."

"That would be greatly appreciated," he said. "And I won't let anybody know you were here, either."

"Thank you," she answered sheepishly.

Even though she had stepped completely out of line, he was kind and courteous toward her. He really was a brilliant man. She understood what it was that Daya saw in him.

"Well, I guess I'll be on my way then, and I'll let you enjoy the rest of your evening," she said, getting up from her seat.

"I'll try my best," he teased.

As Avery left his house, she felt satisfied with how she had handled the conversation. Without a plan, she had successfully done what she had promised not to do. But it had made her feel better, and that was all that mattered.

Charles would possibly be upset, but he had no reason to find out about it. If the mayor kept his word, the entire conversation would forever remain between the two of them.

Just as her car pulled into her driveway, she remembered the rogue bird that she'd left in her dining room. She pressed the back of her head against her seat and closed her eyes.

What am I going to walk into?

She didn't have much choice but to go in and deal with it. It was only a few hours until the women of the Stammtisch would arrive for dinner. So, she took a deep breath and readied herself for what she was certain would be an awful scene.

When she entered the house, the first thing she noted was that Sprinkles was far too quiet. In fact, he was completely silent. That greatly worried her. She tiptoed through the house and approached the dining room.

When she opened the door and peered inside, she saw something she was not at all expecting. On the ground, next to the dining table, lay Sprinkles, completely asleep and exhausted from chasing the bird all morning.

The bird was walking proudly across the countertop, pecking here and there at something Avery couldn't quite see. She was just grateful Sprinkles wasn't a good enough hunter to have caught the bird. With a clearer mind, Avery got a towel and threw it over the bird, after which she carried it safely outside.

It'd been a long time since Avery had grilled up some steak. Le Blanc Cellars had just released a new Sangiovese and it would be the perfect pairing to share with her favorite Stammtisch friends.

The night was cheerful as the group of women enjoyed a freshly cooked meal and many decent glasses of wine. The table had erupted into laughter as Avery recounted the dog training event the day before.

"I tell you that Brie is amazing, and she had a ton of energy," Avery said. "She trained the dogs in the military. She said she served with the mayor."

"Oh yeah," Eleanor added. "I remember now about her and the mayor. That was a lot of drama, wasn't it?"

"Drama?" Avery asked.

"Yeah, when the mayor's wife left, everybody suspected it was perhaps because he was having an affair with Brie," Eleanor explained.

"I remember!" piped Deb. "But when it turned out that Brie was, in fact, in the process of marrying somebody else, everyone sort of dropped those suspicions."

"Yep! I guess his wife was the one with the affair, it seems," Eleanor said, shaking her head.

"What makes you think there was ever any kind of affair?" Avery asked. It amused her that the world was still under the impression that a sudden split had to, almost certainly, be caused by an affair.

"Well," Deb said with a shrug. "Why else would you leave suddenly in the middle of the night and never come back?"

"That's what happened?" Tiffany asked, shocked. "I didn't realize it was quite that dramatic!"

"Yeah!" Deb said, raising her glass to her lips. "She barely even took anything with her. She took her clothes, makeup, and her little dog. That sounds like an angry woman to me."

"Or someone who's afraid," Eleanor said.

"Afraid of the mayor?" Deb laughed. "That's like being afraid of a kitten!"

She wasn't wrong. As far as anybody in the town was concerned, the mayor was completely harmless, and incredibly well-loved.

"I mean, there's no doubt he's wonderful," Avery agreed. "But why then would she leave that way?"

"Because she's having an affair!" Deb said. "Isn't it clear? She left to be with another man. She must have been planning it for months!"

It felt wrong to be discussing such a private part of Mayor Oswald's life when nobody there even really knew him. It was town gossip, but Avery figured it was normal. He was, after all, a public figure.

"I have to admit," Avery said. "That does sound as if there was something unsavory going on. Sounds like an affair to me! But I refuse to believe it was on the mayor's side."

"Poor Brie," Camille eventually said. "It tore her friendship with the mayor apart. Even though there was never any proof of the affair, some members of the town had missed the memo and would call her incredibly rude names when they saw her in the street."

Avery shook her head. She couldn't imagine what that would be like. Brie had seemed like a wonderful woman, and she would never call her any cruel names.

"Never mind all this gossip talk," Camille said. "Eleanor, how are things between you and the doctor?"

Eleanor began to blush slightly, and it reminded Avery of when they had spoken months before. Eleanor had told her she would never consider getting into another relationship after her husband had died. Soon after, she met the new town vet, and they had been dating ever since.

They were happy, and it made Avery sometimes wonder whether she would ever move past the death of James enough to spend her life with another person. She and James had shared everything together. They'd loved the same movies and had the same favorite food. It had seemed almost impossible for them to be so similar and get along so well. She was certain she could never find anything like that again.

"Well," Eleanor said quietly. "He asked me to marry him."

There was a loud gasp around the table as everyone waited patiently for Eleanor to continue.

"He said that since we already see each other every day, we might as well," she said. "I mean, if I'm not staying the night at his house, he is staying the night at mine, and we spend every waking moment together."

"So, did you agree?" Deb asked.

Eleanor shook her head. "On one condition," she said. "I don't want to leave my house. I have many memories there that I am not yet ready to leave behind."

"Oh my gosh, I can't believe you've waited this long to say something," Camille laughed.

"It felt terrible making conditions with him, but I couldn't leave that part of my life that easily," Eleanor said. "I told him he should move into my house."

The rest of the group glanced across the table at each other. Nobody was quite sure if she was telling the truth or kidding. It was exactly the kind of joke that Eleanor would tell.

"So, what did he say?" Deb asked cautiously.

"He agreed," Eleanor said with a smile. "Besides, I think it will be great having a vet in the house!"

"When did he ask?" Camille asked, leaning forward with excitement.

Eleanor let out a loud laugh. "Last week!"

Another loud gasp cannoned around the table as some of the women rose to their feet to give Eleanor a congratulatory hug.

"He proposed last week, and this is the first we're hearing about it?!" Deb shouted excitedly. "Why didn't you tell us?"

"I've been a little busy," Eleanor responded with her cheeks turning bright pink.

"I bet you have!" Deb cheered, topping up Eleanor's glass with a bit more wine.

By the time the women left her house, Avery was smiling widely. It had been a successful day. She had done what was necessary to put her own heart and mind at peace, her friends were happy and sharing good news, and it had been a successful year for the business.

All of it had made her feel much better about how things were between her and Charles. Granted, she had a little bit of guilt for everything he'd had to go through, only for her to confess to the crime anyway. But he had acted on his own terms, and so had she.

Avery stepped out onto the porch with a cup of tea to admire the stars. She wasn't really sure why she had done it; it was the first time she had done it in years. It was something that she had often done with her father and then after that with James.

The sky was clear, and the stars were bright. The air was cold, but it only made the warm tea taste so much better.

And when Avery finally crawled into bed, it took her no more than a few seconds before she was fast asleep. Not even the sound of Sprinkles snoring loudly at her feet would wake her.

Chapter Eighteen

Although the rain was beautiful, it only made Avery feel sad. She wasn't sure if it was the gray skies or the fact that she couldn't go for a morning walk, but she wasn't as excited about the start of the wet season as the rest of her group of friends.

The one thing that did keep her cheerful was the knowledge that once the rain had passed, beautiful plants would make their appearance. Although it was still morning, she had convinced herself that she deserved a day in bed with her favorite movies.

That was until she received a text from Charles that he wouldn't be at work. He had become ill. Charles had never been out sick, so Avery had never needed to make a plan for when he wasn't there. She had nobody to call, so she knew she'd have to fill in for him.

Avery typed out a quick message to Charles, instructing him to stay in bed and get better as soon as possible, and then dragged herself back out of bed to get ready to work.

By the time she unlocked the wine room, it was already an hour past opening hour. It didn't make much of a difference, though. With the rain, she wasn't expecting too many customers that day. Avery put on some music and started preparing the wine room. She was halfway through her routine when she received another message from Charles.

Just got the news that all charges against me regarding the photographs have been dropped. Apparently, someone confessed, but they won't tell me who. You promised you'd stay out of it.

Avery's stomach sank. She turned off the music and slumped back against the wine bar. Technically, the mayor had kept his promise and hadn't told anybody it was her. But Charles knew that it was her, and he was smart enough to piece it together.

Despite knowing what she had done was right and being happy Charles was no longer blamed for it, she still felt waves of guilt wash over her throughout the day. She had felt so guilty that she didn't even know what to say to him. So, instead, she said nothing at all. Which wasn't a good option either. By the time the work day had ended, and she was loading Sprinkles in the car for his next training session, it was too late. She had gone so long without responding to him, that anything she said to him would have sounded like an afterthought.

Then it occurred to her that perhaps he wasn't ill at all. There was a possibility he was so upset with her that he simply didn't want to see her that day, which was fair. But it made her feel awful. And the fact that she felt so awful about it made her confused. Then, the fact that she felt confused about it made her irritable. *Why are you so concerned? You're his boss, and you're a grown woman. You can do whatever you want.* She needed to run her feelings by somebody else. So, she called Tiffany on her Bluetooth system.

"Hello?" Tiffany's voice crackled through the speakers.

"Can you hear me?" Avery shouted. "Hello? Hello?"

"I can hear you!" Tiffany called back. "Stop shouting! Why are you shouting?"

"Oh," Avery laughed. "I've never used the Bluetooth in my car. I wasn't sure how it worked."

"Welcome to the new age!" Tiffany teased. "Now, what is so urgent that you have to phone me while you're driving? In the rain, might I add?"

Avery gave Tiffany a brief summary of what had happened between the mayor and Charles and her recent conversation with the mayor as well. Tiffany was the only person she could talk to about it because she was the only other person who knew about the photographs.

"You didn't need to take all the blame," Tiffany reprimanded her. "I could have gone with you."

"It was never my intention to clear my name," Avery admitted. "Charles only took the blame because I might have faced jail time."

"Oh, I see," Tiffany said. "And you think he knows you've spoken to the mayor?"

"It's the only conclusion that he could possibly get to!"

"So, what exactly is the problem?" she asked. "I thought it would be good if his name was cleared?"

"I feel guilty, and I'm frustrated that I feel guilty," Avery explained. "Something about it all just gives me a bad feeling, and I can't figure out why."

"I mean, that seems normal to me," Tiffany teased.

"Well, Charles is my friend, and I'm his boss," Avery continued. "And I know I should feel bad, but there's something else. I was really upset with him when he called in sick this morning. How can I be upset if he is ill? It happens! It's normal!"

There was a short bit of silence on the other end of the line, and then she heard Tiffany wheeze with laughter. It took a good few minutes before Tiffany had composed herself again. "I'm sorry that I'm laughing," Tiffany said through sniffs. "It's just that sometimes you can be *so* dumb!"

"I don't understand," Avery said, unimpressed.

"You miss him, you idiot," Tiffany said through more laughter.

Almost immediately, Avery did feel like an idiot. But only because Tiffany had been right. How could she not have figured out that she missed him? The moment Tiffany had spoken the words, Avery knew it was the truth, and all of her emotions fell back into place.

"You're right," Avery said in shock. "How odd."

"It's not odd," Tiffany said. "You guys get along. You're usually joking and laughing together, and now you haven't been. But I'm sure things will come right soon, and you guys will joke together again."

"I hope so because I don't like missing him," Avery said.

"Listen, I have to go," Tiffany said.

In the background, she could hear Tiffany open her front door and greet someone before ending the call. Avery sighed and did her best to swallow her embarrassment. She was sure that Tiffany would be teasing her about that phone call for at least the next few months.

There were more dogs in training that day than there had been the previous time. And this time, the owners were expected to join in. Brie seemed a lot less friendly when

Avery was on the receiving end of her military-style training.

The wet weather meant they had to do the session in the school gymnasium. Avery had hoped never to find herself back at her old school again, but for the first time ever, it was an enjoyable experience. Sprinkles had been learning fast, and it felt good to do something completely different from her normal routine.

"You guys did well," Brie said as the training ended.

She took a seat next to Avery and patted Sprinkles on the head.

"Thank you," Avery said. "You're a tough coach!"

Brie laughed. "Mayor Oswald said that once too. I used to think I had to be tough on the military dogs because they played such an important role. But I've come to realize that every dog plays an important role. Every single one."

Avery smiled at that thought. "I've been meaning to ask you," she said. "What exactly do military dogs do?" Brie's face dropped at the mention of it, and Avery immediately regretted the question.

"You don't have to answer if you don't want to," Avery said.

"No, that's alright," Brie smiled. "It's an interesting question."

Brie took a large sip from her water bottle. "The dogs are trained to save lives," she answered. "Each mission is different, but sometimes they are sent to detect bombs and that kind of thing. However, when I left, Mayor Oswald was pushing for a new type of training. He felt that the dogs could be used to create distractions, drawing the enemy away from the real threat."

"That's fascinating," Avery said. "I would never have guessed."

"They were pretty successful too!" Brie said. "Especially

the dogs that were part of Oswald's missions."

"He led missions with dogs in them?" Avery asked. It felt like every new bit of information she received about the mayor was more fascinating than the last.

"Yes!" Brie said excitedly. "He was an excellent strategist. Hardly any of his missions were unsuccessful. He had a really good way of distracting the enemy in order to get his men through and back alive."

"That sounds really impressive," Avery said softly. "Especially for such a gentle man."

"He is a gentle man now," Brie said with a cheeky smile. "But he could be dangerous when he needed to be."

The conversation came to an end before Avery could ask any more questions. Brie turned her attention to another pet parent who had a list of questions for her.

Avery woke the exhausted Sprinkles and dragged him back into the car. At that moment, she was grateful for the rain on her skin as it cooled her down and washed away the sweat from what felt like a parent-pet boot camp.

As soon as she got home, she thought about Charles again. She had to say something to him. People like to know when they're missed, and she was certain he was no different in that regard. But when she typed out the words, they just felt foolish. And yet, she couldn't just stay quiet completely. If the only other option was to be cheesy, that would have to be it. So, she typed her original message out anyway. *I saw something funny today that I know would have made you laugh. I'm sorry for the trouble I have caused, but I was only doing what I thought was right. I hope that you'll see that one day. I miss you.*

She wasn't sure what she expected him to say in response. But when he said nothing, she didn't know what to do. Despite her exhaustion, she could barely sleep. His silence was loud enough to keep her wide awake.

Chapter Nineteen

Avery was unfortunately underdressed as she raced across the lawn in her sleeping shorts and shirt, an excited Sprinkles running ahead of her. One of her dish towels was secured in his jaw, and as far as Sprinkles was concerned, they had just started a fun game.

"Give me that!" she yelled as she raced after the golden retriever.

By the time she had successfully rescued the towel, she was grateful for the cool air and damp grass. She stood a moment to catch her breath before going back inside. Sprinkles, on the other hand, waited a moment to roll around in the dirt before making his way back into the house to lie down on the freshly cleaned sofa.

Avery sighed. "You're lucky you're so darn cute," she mumbled as she chased the dog back outside.

Somewhere in the depths of her home, she could hear her phone vibrating like mad. When she'd finally found it, she saw multiple missed calls from Deb. Avery wasn't sure what had happened, but usually, Deb only phoned when there was some serious town gossip. And she knew it was best to call her back and save herself the string of messages that would arrive if she didn't.

"Hi Deb, what's up?" Avery said when her call was answered.

"Did you hear the news?"

It was a typical conversation starter for Deb.

"You'll have to be a little more specific than that," Avery said with a chuckle.

"The postman, you know, the one with the Velcro shoes?" Deb said.

"I know the one," Avery said as she dried the morning mist from her face. Her hair was damp from chasing Sprinkles.

"Well, he's been diagnosed with arthritis. Apparently, he won't be able to work much longer as the postman!" Deb spoke as if it was the biggest news of the century, and Avery was just amazed she was able to find that kind of information.

"That's terrible news," Avery said blankly, but her mind was running a million miles per hour. His diagnosis and the ending of his long career certainly would have explained why he was behaving strangely the last time that the mayor had spent time with him. He would have been in pain and likely awaiting results from the tests. With his behavior explained, his likelihood of being a suspect began to fade. Still, she couldn't be too certain.

"I just think he should get a second opinion," Deb continued. Avery could tell that Deb was gearing up for a longer conversation than Avery had the energy for. So, she excused herself to get ready for the day and ended the conversation as quickly as she could after twenty minutes.

She was about to leave her phone on the counter when she noticed she had a large number of messages waiting. She was in no mood to read them but knew if she didn't, she would spend the entirety of her shower wondering what they were about.

So, she gave in and checked. There were multiple messages on the Stammtisch group text about the postman's unfortunate diagnosis, a message from her mother about the speed of the Internet, and a message from Tiffany.

Avery responded to the rest of the messages first before opening Tiffany's chat. Tiffany was the kind of friend who only ever messaged if it was something of importance. So, she made sure she was ready for something serious before opening the message.

Just saw the woman with the heron tattoo at the grocery store. Feels weird to walk past her, knowing what I know. Can't believe she isn't in jail.

It came as no surprise to Avery that Daya was seen around town. Charles had explained that they could only detain her for a short time. The fact that she was out of jail meant that the police never did find any evidence to suggest she had been involved.

Avery wondered what the mayor had done after she had been sent home. Had they seen each other? Had he called things off with her? It really wasn't any of her business, but after everything she knew about the mayor, she worried about him.

She had a mind to message Tiffany back and ask if Daya looked sad. That way, she could convince herself it was because the mayor had dumped her. But it really was none of her business, and she had already gotten far too involved with his personal life. So, she resisted the urge and instead showered to get ready for the day. Charles had called in sick again, so Avery was working the tasting room. The rain had stopped, and she was certain the wine tastings would be busier again and looked forward to the distraction.

Charles' message to let her know he wouldn't be in to work had come through in an email. He still hadn't responded to her text, and it left Avery with an unending feeling of emptiness in her stomach and chest. She wasn't a fan of the way it made her feel. She would rather feel nothing than be upset that her employee was missing yet another day of work. Instead, she felt sad and a little bit alone. In reality, she felt completely lost when it came to Charles.

She had no idea exactly how upset he was with her or how to make things right with him. All she could do was accept responsibility for how things were and hope the answers would come to her.

She had her doubts, though. She'd never been good in those situations. In fact, until recently, she had hardly any friends, so situations like that had never been a reality for her. She wondered how silence from Charles could make her feel so alone when she was still surrounded by so many others.

When the workday was over, Avery headed to her home to have a cup of coffee. As she poured the steaming coffee into a bright red mug, she opened the chat box between her and Charles for what she was certain was the hundredth time that day. There was still no response.

The sun was starting to hang low in the atmosphere, and a soft rain had started up again. When she turned to face the window, she saw that the sky had taken on a soft purple color. She knew that the surrounding vineyards would look beautiful in the rain.

She abandoned the cup of coffee and jumped in the car to go for a drive. There had to be something that would cheer her up, and she figured a drive would help clear her head.

Avery envied Deb a little when she felt so consumed by her thoughts and wondered if it was pleasant to be so consumed by the lives of others. Perhaps it would mean that her own life wouldn't cause her so much stress. Maybe that was why Deb liked to gossip so much. Avery could hardly imagine being so focused on the lives of others that her own thoughts were silenced. What bliss.

As Avery's car peaked the top of the hill, she gasped at the beautiful view. The soft purple sky had deep gray clouds rolling in. The vines seemed to be heavy with rain, making the hills look like something out of a movie.

The swallows danced through the sky, creating liquid forms as they enjoyed their last bit of flight for the day. The roads were quiet, and for a moment, so was her mind. In the windows of all the houses, she could see warm glows as everyone prepared themselves for a colder night.

She imagined what she would make for dinner and that perhaps she would make a fire and enjoy a movie and a glass of wine. The drive was doing the trick, and Avery could feel the peace creeping back into her bones.

Small wafts of mist were creeping between the vineyards like a slow smoke machine. Suddenly Avery felt so small compared to the natural world.

Stop worrying. The vines do not worry, and yet they are fruitful. It occurred to her that all of her worrying and sleepless nights had made no difference to the outcome of reality. So what was the point?

The rain poured harder, and Avery knew that her drive would soon have to come to an end. Something about the vineyards and the weather had filled her up again. For the first time in days, she felt as if everything was actually alright.

Just as the rain had washed the dust off the vines so that they could flourish, it had cleansed Avery's own mind of its stagnant thoughts so that she could find relief. It didn't matter how long it took Charles to get back to her, she knew that he would, and all she had to do was wait. It didn't matter how many times she tried to imagine what he might say; in the end, it would be different, and she would find a way to respond.

Avery turned her car around to head home just as the rain started pelting down at its hardest. Visibility was low, and the roads were a little too wet for her preference. So, she dropped all thought of anything and concentrated solely on the road in front of her.

She was only a few blocks from home, waiting at an intersection. The visibility was worse, and she couldn't help but feel that she shouldn't drive just yet. Still, she looked in both directions and saw no headlights heading her way.

The vines don't worry. So, don't worry. Avery relaxed and made her way across the intersection. She was about halfway across when the sound of another car snuck up on her. Just as she glanced to her right, she saw a car with its headlights off, traveling at a speed that was faster than her reaction time. She slammed on the brakes and swerved, but it was no use. The front of her car just clipped the tail end of the speeding car. She saw the rain kick out from under the wheels as the other car came to a quick and dangerous stop.

"You can't be serious," Avery said as she put her hazards on and put her car in park.

Chapter Twenty

"Are you kidding me?" Avery said as she looked out at the car she had just hit. "Now I have to get out and get soaked."

She peered out the window, wishing there was some other way they could go about it. She should have trusted her gut. She should have believed the worry that had brewed in her mind just before her foot had touched the accelerator. "Always trust your gut," she mumbled as she reached for the door handle.

Avery did her best to cover her head with her jacket as she climbed out of her car and into the pouring rain. Even though the situation wasn't the best, the rain actually felt good against her skin. It seemed to cool her frustration.

She walked around her car to inspect the damage. She wasn't sure who she had hit. It was a car she didn't quite recognize, which was better. *At least I didn't hit a friend. Imagine how embarrassing that would be.*

The rain had made it a little hard to see, but she could see a few scratches on her car. Thankfully, it was nothing too serious, but she was sure it would still be pretty expensive. So, she walked over to see what the other car looked like. It had considerably more damage than her own, something she was certain the car's owner wouldn't be too pleased about.

"That's what happens when you're driving like a maniac," she said loudly enough that she was certain the driver could hear her.

Nobody had stepped out of the car yet, which didn't seem fair to her. She was soaking wet, and the other driver stayed nice and dry in their car. Surely they didn't think that the accident was her fault? She trudged over to inspect the damage on the other car and heard two doors slam. "I don't have time for this," a familiar voice said.

Avery knew who it was before she even looked up. She didn't want to believe that it could be him. Of all the people in the town she could have hit with her car, she'd hit the one man whose boundaries she had already crossed far too many times.

"Mayor Oswald, are you alright?" she asked as she walked toward him.

"Avery?" he said, staring at her through the rain. "This rain made it so difficult to see. I am so sorry!"

Avery was smiling at him when Daya walked up and wrapped her arm in his. She stared at the two of them for a moment, quite clearly still a couple. The mayor kept his eyes down as Avery tried to understand why he would stay with a woman who likely murdered her husband.

"Are you okay?" Daya asked, and Avery thought that she would be sick. She simply stared at the woman with such a bad taste in her mouth that she was certain it was showing on her face.

"Is your car alright?" Daya asked again, smiling at Avery.

The mayor shifted uncomfortably on his feet as Daya

went to inspect the damage on both cars. Avery simply continued to stare in disbelief as she tried to piece it all together.

Then it occurred to her that perhaps he was in danger. She had seemed like the type of person who would take a man hostage. After all, she seemed perfectly willing to murder a man. Avery's heart started racing. She decided that Daya had to have been driving. It explained the speed of the car and the lack of headlights. She was trying to make a run for it, and she was taking the mayor with her. She must have been driving.

Daya returned to Mayor Oswald's side and tugged on his sleeve.

"It doesn't seem all too bad," she said to him. "Of course, it is unfortunate, but I'm sure it will all be worked out."

"I didn't see you there," the mayor said to Avery.

"You were driving?" she asked, glancing between him and Daya.

"Yes," he admitted with a forced chuckle. "I suppose I wasn't behaving quite as I should in weather like this. I'm willing to admit fault. I was driving way too fast!"

"Oh," Avery said, still uncertain. "Are you in a hurry? Is everything alright?"

"Yes, everything's just fine," he said with a strange, joyful tone to his voice. "We were just not paying attention. I'm just glad nobody got hurt."

"Yes, thank goodness!" Daya added.

He was driving?

She glanced at their car and noticed that there were bags packed in the back seat, along with what looked to be a tent and some blankets.

"Are you going away?" she asked, puzzled.

"Yes," Daya said cheerfully. "We decided we needed a break, and we're going away for the weekend."

"Not too far from here," the mayor added. "We just thought we'd get some space from everything for a day or two."

The mayor chuckled again, and it made Avery feel completely uneasy. Something about the way he was smiling and laughing seemed so odd to her. He seemed nothing like the man she had met at the barbecue or the man she had spoken to at his house.

As the mist began to wrap around their feet, Avery couldn't help but think that he looked as if it suited him. As if he was made for the gray, stormy background against which he stood. The way Daya looked at him seemed to be with comfort and Avery understood that a look like that only came from being incredibly close.

They're way too comfortable.

Then she realized that perhaps it wasn't his behavior at the car crash that she was confused about. Maybe it was his behavior that day at his house that she had misunderstood. He had been calm—a little too calm.

Initially, she was convinced that he was merely shocked. But now that Avery saw him still intertwined with Daya, she felt that perhaps he was a little too unconcerned about her potentially being a murderer.

She thought about everything that she knew about him. The stories about him being in the military, for instance. She had thought it made him a good man, but it might only mean he was strong. She had always understood that being in the military made you an excellent man. But she knew stories of men who were forever changed in a bad way because of it. It had never occurred to her that the mayor might have come out of the military with an innate ability to be unaffected by the good and bad of the world.

That would have been why he was such a good police officer. Who was she kidding? He was a politician. Few politicians were truly good men, and she had led herself to believe that Mayor Oswald was one. But why had his wife left in the middle of the night? And why had the friendship between him and Brie soured?

And she had understood that it just meant that he was good at his job. But being a good strategist in the military is different than being a good strategist in a football game. He was good at coming up with strategies that cost the lives of others, not just their money.

He had planned to use the dogs to create distractions. Strategy was what he had been really good at. He was excellent at creating distractions that could send an entire troop of enemy soldiers searching in the wrong direction.

She thought back to the first conversation she'd had with him and all the reasons why it had initially bothered her. He had lied about not attending the first day of the festival when she was certain she had seen him there.

She looked at him and knew that those were the same glasses that she had seen. In an instant, all of his behavior fell into place. His conversations, his calmness, his eagerness to have the photographs covered up, and why he had been so scarce at the festival. All of it. Avery's feet felt as if they had turned to lead, as if she could never move again.

"Are you sure you're alright?" Daya asked again.

She looked at the woman with the heron tattoo and saw her through a different lens. Why had she been so cheerful that day at the coffee shop? Why could they find no evidence to use against her? Had she done this before? Then it dawned on Avery that they found no evidence against Daya because it never existed.

"I'm alright," Avery answered, forcing a smile. "Just a little cold." Avery needed to think fast. She needed to decide what she was going to do because every piece of the puzzle had finally fallen into place for her.

Mayor Oswald had murdered the man at the festival. Everything else had simply been a distraction, part of his strategy. And now, he was trying to flee.

Chapter Twenty-One

Avery's head was spinning as she tried to comprehend what she was now certain was the truth. She had been so hell-bent on proving who the murderer was that she hadn't even bothered to look at what had been staring her right in the face.

They were going to get away, and she was the only person who knew about it. She was the only person who knew about any of it. She had to do something to make sure they didn't get away. She couldn't follow them since they would certainly notice. Asking them where they were going wouldn't work either. She had been staring at them for so long that she was certain the mayor could tell she had figured it out. She needed to do something to make it seem like she was just going to carry on with her day. She needed them to believe that they would get away with it and that they would be able to escape. But there was only one person she trusted enough to ask for help in that situation, and he hadn't been speaking to her. Still, it was her best hope and the only plan she could come up with at the time.

"Let me just see if I can take some photographs," she

said with a smile. "Then I can leave you to it, and the two of you can enjoy your time away." She pulled out her phone and took some photographs of everything. Then, before slipping the phone back into her pocket, she dialed Charles' number and hoped he would answer. He had no reason to answer her call, but she could still hope that he would.

The rain had let up just enough that it was no longer that difficult to see or hear anything. Just to make sure, she looked at the mayor again, doing her best to assess his body language. He certainly didn't seem like a man that was there against his will.

In fact, he seemed to be impatient. She watched as he checked his watch every few seconds, his foot tapping slightly against the roadside. He wanted to leave and was in a hurry. Daya, on the other hand, didn't seem to behave as if anything was wrong.

The first call went unanswered. So, she pulled her phone out again.

"I see there's an angle that I missed," she said with a nervous laugh. "Let me just get that angle." She snapped the photograph and texted Charles.

Pick up. It's urgent. But don't say anything when you answer. Just listen.

Then, she gave it a few minutes before dialing his number again and holding her phone at waist level with her. She needed to make sure it looked natural. She also needed to see if Charles answered her call.

She was about to give up the notion entirely when she saw the screen change. He had answered. She waited a moment to see the call had been connected for a second or two before she proceeded with the next part of her plan.

She took a step closer to the mayor and Daya. "You

know the roads a little better than I do, mayor," she said loudly. "Where would you say it is that we are?"

"We're at the intersection between Jeffrey's Boulevard and Church Street," he said with a puzzled look.

"Oh! Of course, I can never remember the street names!" Avery said cheerfully. "I just want to make sure that I can give the correct information to my insurance."

"That's okay. Let's get it all sorted, and then we can be on our way," he said with a forced smile as he checked his watch again.

"I didn't see you coming!" she said loud enough for Charles to hear. "How unfortunate that we should meet again this way."

The last sentence clearly made the mayor uncomfortable, as the previous time they had been together, Avery had been at his house to warn him about his girlfriend.

"You two know each other?" Daya asked.

"We've met a few times," Avery said calmly. "Only recently."

"I've never met you before," Daya said, taking a step forward.

"No, you haven't," Avery said with a smile, glancing at the mayor. "I'm Avery." Avery took a step toward her to shake her hand. All she could hope was that Charles was able to hear what was being said.

"I'm Daya," she greeted with a friendly smile.

"I'm so sorry about all of this," Avery said and noticed the mayor roll his eyes. "It is tedious, but as soon as we get the details out of the way, then the two of you can continue on to wherever it was that you were in such a hurry to get to."

"Of course!" the mayor said, forcing a smile. "Again, as I said, I was driving way too fast. I really am sorry."

"Nobody's hurt, and that's all that matters," Avery

said. "I am sorry that I've interrupted your weekend away. It sure looks like you're packed for more than a weekend, though." Avery laughed to make it seem as if she had simply been teasing them both. She needed to act as if none of it really bothered her. One of the two people in front of her had no problem murdering for their own personal gain. It still wasn't clear to her if they had worked together, though.

"If you don't mind, Avery. I'd like to hurry things up. I need to be checked in before a certain time," Mayor Oswald said, still doing his best to remain friendly.

"Of course not," Avery said. "Let me just make a note of what the damage really is, and you can be on your way. Where is it you're heading?"

The mayor and Daya kept completely quiet.

"I don't mean to pry," Avery said. "It's just that I've been meaning to get away for a while, and I can't seem to find anywhere worth going. I thought that perhaps you could suggest a place for me." The two glanced uneasily at each other.

"It's sort of a surprise for Daya," the mayor said, creating yet another brilliant diversion.

"Yes," Daya said eagerly. "I have no idea where we're going! Isn't that romantic?"

The rain was still falling softly, and Avery would have loved nothing more than to be inside where it was warm. The fingers that gripped her phone were so cold she didn't know if she could move them anymore.

She glanced at her phone and saw Charles was still connected to the call. She could only assume that it meant that he was listening. She didn't know if he would understand what was going on, but she had no choice but to hope it would work.

"Did you hear that the postman has arthritis?" she

asked, making conversation in an attempt to stall the events of the day.

All that still bothered her were the stones.

"Which postman?" the mayor asked.

"The one with the Velcro shoes," Avery said, realizing that it was a ridiculous way to identify a man. "You said he was behaving strangely the last time you saw him, maybe that's why."

"Ah," the mayor said as he began to pace slowly. "That would be Evan."

"Evan," Avery laughed. "You know, it's terrible. People like Evan are such a part of my life, yet I never thought to ask his name."

"Yes," the mayor said dryly. "Perhaps you should get to know people a little better around here."

Avery wasn't sure if it was a threat. Had he implied that she should have waited to know him better before rushing to his house to warn him against Daya? Had she scared the mayor off? Had her visit with him been why he was fleeing in the first place?

"You're right," Avery said, making direct eye contact with him.

"You never know," Daya said, joining a conversation she didn't truly understand. "Perhaps you would find that you and Evan get along really well. That happened to me and the mayor."

The mayor cleared his throat and shot Daya a look. She seemed to understand what he meant by it. Clearly, the two of them had been together longer than anyone had originally suspected.

Avery thought about Daya's husband and how he had tried to warn them that she had done it. She thought about the stones and the mayor's lies about his whereabouts. All of it made her angry. It needed to end.

She wasn't sure what she was going to do, but she knew she couldn't let them leave. Still, it was hard to know if she was in any danger. "Right, well," Avery said, pretending to be satisfied with her assessment of the damage. "It seems as if your car has had more damage than mine."

"That's unfortunate," the mayor said. "Thankfully, it is still drivable, so we can still get to our destination in time."

"Wouldn't you like to take note of the damage?" Avery asked. "For insurance purposes? I can send it to you if you like. What's your number?"

"It's really no problem," the mayor said. "Just tell me which insurance company you're with, and I'll make sure to settle all the costs."

"Don't be ridiculous," Avery protested.

The mayor was clearly willing to go to any length to make sure that they didn't waste any more time. "No, really," he continued. "I insist. It was my fault. I was going too fast. Please, don't worry about it."

Avery was playing a losing game and wasn't sure what to do. The call was still connected, but she was ready to call it a night when a message came through from Charles.

I can hear you. Keep going.

Chapter Twenty-Two

She didn't know what Charles planned on doing about it, but Avery was certain she was staring the real murderer in the face. And she was even more certain that he was about to leave. She had stalled as much as she possibly could but was running out of excuses to keep him there.

"Right, well, as soon as you've done your checks," she said. "I guess we can all carry on with our journeys. Where did you say you were going?"

"It's a surprise," the mayor said, walking toward his driver's side door.

"D-don't you want to take some photographs?" she asked.

Mayor Oswald was growing impatient. She could tell by the way he continuously clenched his jaw. He had the driver's side door already partly open and took a deep breath to calm himself down.

"Why don't you just send me what you have?" he suggested. "We really are in a bit of a hurry. I don't want to miss the check-in."

Avery was beginning to panic. She couldn't let him get away. She needed to do something, anything to make him stay. She was willing to put almost anything on the line, and there was only one thing she could think to do.

She would confront him, and she would confront him well enough that he would react exactly as he should and stay to confront her too. It wasn't a perfect plan, and she wasn't sure it would work, but she knew he was angry, and that could work to her benefit if she played her cards right.

"You killed him, didn't you?" she said as loudly as possible.

The mayor paused and turned to face her, his expression cold and hard. "What did you say?" he said stiffly.

"This whole time, I thought it was her," Avery said, pointing at Daya. "But you killed her husband, didn't you?"

The mayor abandoned his efforts at climbing into his car, and Avery knew that her plan had worked. She just hoped that whatever Charles was doing, he was doing it fast. She could be in danger, and she hadn't thought far enough ahead for that.

"I would suggest that you stop talking," he said through clenched teeth as he approached her.

"What is she talking about?" Daya said, joining them in the rain.

"You said that you weren't there on the first day of the festival," Avery explained. "But I know I saw you there. You were standing behind a building. I thought it was odd. And I couldn't understand why you had lied and said that you weren't there when I saw you."

"Be careful, Avery," the mayor warned again.

"And now you're trying to run, aren't you?" she said. "This is no weekend away. Who leaves for the weekend at this time of day?"

"You said you weren't going to be at the festival that

day," Daya said. "You didn't want to make things uncomfortable for Kevin and me."

Finally, Avery learned the victim's name.

"I saw him there," Avery said to Daya. "Just a few hours before your husband was found dead."

"You have no proof," said the mayor. "This is ridiculous."

"No, but I know you're an excellent strategist," she said. "And I know you used to train dogs to create a distraction, isn't that right? And I've just realized that Daya was that distraction."

"What is she talking about?" Daya said, approaching the mayor with caution.

"What was it?" Avery continued. "Did you want to enjoy his insurance money, too? Were the divorce proceedings taking a little too long? Why did you do it?"

"Enough!" the mayor shouted. He was red in the face from rage. "Why couldn't you just butt out like you were instructed to do?"

"And the stones," Avery continued. "They puzzled me at first. But you knew how uncommon they were, and you knew how busy that would keep the police in the investigation. So, you took some that day when you were at Evan's house, when you say he was acting strangely."

"What are you talking about? What did you do?!" Daya shouted through tears of rage.

"I secured a life for us," the mayor said. "He was going to take everything from you. I couldn't stand by and watch it happen."

Avery nearly cheered with excitement when he started talking. But one look at him told her he was angry enough to murder again. She wanted to step away from him, but she needed Charles to hear it all. A glance at her phone told her he was still on the line.

"You placed the stones there as a distraction," Avery said with a coy smile. "Why, though? Why would you frame the very woman you were aiming to protect?"

"Because she's clean, you idiot," he snarled. "You think you're so smart, but you couldn't figure out the simplest part of it all. I knew they would find no evidence on her. She was the only lead they had. It would buy us enough time to get out of town and start our lives together."

Daya stared at him in disbelief. Tears streamed down her cheeks as her legs gave way beneath her, and she collapsed to her knees. "Please tell me it isn't true," she cried.

"You were never supposed to find out about any of this," he said. "If it wasn't for this meddling woman always sticking her nose where it doesn't belong, we'd have been out of here by now, and all of this could have been left behind."

"Why would you do this to me?" Daya cried.

"Because I love you," the mayor said, his shoulders dropping. "I killed innocent soldiers on opposing sides because I love my country. I killed criminals while on duty because I love my citizens. I killed Kevin because I love you."

"Why the stones?" Avery asked. "Wouldn't they have looked into her anyway?"

"It's no secret that our police force isn't the greatest," the mayor laughed. "I just needed to make sure they looked in the wrong direction. But they never even found the stones! It almost hadn't worked. Then, thankfully, you found them!"

"This is insane," Daya sobbed. "This is not what I wanted. They interrogated me for days because of you!"

"But we're free now," the mayor said. "Your name was cleared, just like I knew it would be. And we can leave all of this behind."

"What about her?" Daya asked, pointing in Avery's direction. "She'll talk."

"After everything she's done, nobody will believe her," the mayor laughed.

"I came to you to warn you," Avery said. "I was worried that your girlfriend was a murderer, and I warned you to stay away." Avery glanced over at Daya. "Sorry," she said sheepishly.

"Yes, you did," the mayor smiled. "And it really was very sweet. But it was your meddling that ruined my plan in the first place. They were supposed to accuse her of murder, but our affair was never supposed to come to light."

"Ah," Avery said, wishing Charles would give her some kind of guidance.

"If it weren't for those highly inappropriate photographs of the two of us, my name would have stayed out of this entirely," he shouted.

She couldn't believe his audacity. He blamed her for the failure of his plan, as if she was the bad person in all of this. Meanwhile, he was an actual murderer. Suddenly she wished she had hit them harder with her car.

"And what would have been the reason you disappeared?" Avery asked. "Did you think you could just pack your bags and leave, and it would all be over?"

"Originally, I thought I'd have more time to leave. But, after your photographs, I realized that it would make things more complicated. So, at midnight tonight, those photographs will be leaked. By my own arrangement."

"I don't understand," Avery said.

"Of course you don't," he cried, raising his palms to the sky. "First, the photographs, then the notice of my stepping down as mayor. Nobody will care where I've gone after that."

"You won't get away with this," Avery said.

Despite her fear of being his next victim, she couldn't help but be amused by the irony of the situation. She was using his own strategy of distraction against him. Only, she didn't have a very well-thought-out plan. Hers was being created on the spot.

"What do you think?" he asked. "That anyone would believe you? I've given this town my life. They've always been on my side."

"Not after your scandal comes to light," Avery said. "Do you think they'll still have your back when they see at the photographs of the two of you together?"

"It doesn't matter," he said. "I'll be gone by then. You are nobody to this community. They have no reason to believe a word you say."

She had run out of things to say. The conversation had carried on too long, and she didn't want to risk her safety anymore. So Avery stopped talking and prayed Charles had recorded the phone call.

Chapter Twenty-Three

T he rain had started to pour a lot harder as the mayor walked back to his car. And when Avery glanced at her phone again, she saw that Charles was no longer listening. The call had probably been disconnected due to the weather. She had no idea when it had disconnected or how much of the mayor's confession Charles had heard. And it struck her that maybe it had all been for nothing anyway. But as the mayor turned the key in his ignition, the sky lit up with flashing blue lights.

Cars surrounded them with sirens blaring. And Avery just stood and watched, waves of relief crashing through her. Teams of officers ran from their vehicles toward the mayor's car. And when Avery looked again, both the mayor and Daya were being handcuffed and pushed into police vehicles.

"Avery!" she heard Charles call.

She searched for him through the heavy rain and flashing lights. It was hard to make sense of anything anymore. Then she spotted him. He had called to her from a group of officers who seemed to be asking him a stream of questions.

She took a step toward him when a firm hand wrapped around her arm. "Ma'am, you need to come with us for some questioning," an officer said as he led her toward her vehicle.

"Questioning?" she asked. "Have I done something wrong?"

"No, ma'am," the officer laughed. "We just need an official statement from you. We'd like to get all the details of tonight's event. Once we've got that sorted, you'll be free to return home."

She didn't want to go with the officer. She wanted to go to Charles. She wanted to apologize to him for everything and thank him for coming to her rescue despite it all. But another firm tug at her arm told her she had no choice.

The questions seemed to carry on forever. Every question was followed by a series of follow-up questions. She did her best to answer them all as accurately as possible. By the time they were done, Charles was no longer there.

Avery drove home in silence, in complete shock at the events of the day. She still wasn't entirely sure if it was over. Nobody could tell her if she would be required to testify or what would come next. All she knew was that she was desperate to go home and spend a quiet night with Sprinkles. She was certain that she wouldn't get any sleep either. There was too much adrenaline coursing through her system. How could she be expected to wake up the next day and carry on like normal? *Oh, come on. This is not the worst thing you've been through. And yet, you've managed every day since.*

When she finally made it home, she knew that the only way to distract herself would be to cook a meal. It was way too late for it to make any sense. But she expected it to fill enough of her time. And she counted on that.

Thankfully, she remembered that she had some leftover steaks from when the Stammtisch women were over. Time to repurpose those leftovers into some steak sandwiches. Being in the kitchen, chopping away, and getting her hands dirty was Avery's idea of a perfect distraction.

Avery and Sprinkles shared a tasty dinner together as she ran him through some of the new tricks he'd learned from training with Brie. It wasn't the best distraction, but it cleared her mind of thoughts of the mayor and his murderous plans.

However, her thoughts were now occupied with Charles. He had saved her, and she hadn't even had the chance to talk to him. She wasn't even sure if he wanted to talk. He had been so upset with her, and she couldn't expect him to just drop it all.

She would have to find a way to make it up to him, but she had no idea where to begin.

Was he at the police station? Briefly, she considered going there to see if she could find him. Perhaps he was at home, taking it easy just like she was. She could send him a message, but she wouldn't even know how to start it. Everything that she needed to say to him simply wasn't right for a message. She couldn't be that cold. It wouldn't work.

She was elbow-deep in cleaning the dinner dishes when she heard a familiar knock at the door—three knocks, a pause, and then two knocks. She knew immediately who it was. She rushed to the door and pulled it open.

"Something smells delicious," Charles said with a smile as she opened the door. "And I'm starving." She'd never been so relieved to see Charles with a smile on his face.

"Come in; I'll dish some up for you," she said, stepping aside to let him in. "It's the least I can do."

Charles lifted a box in the air. "I have some cake. Bee Sting. That's your favorite, right?"

"My all-time favorite," Avery said with a grin.

At that moment, she understood that no apology was needed from either of them. And they enjoyed a meal together as if nothing had ever happened.

The birds had only just started chirping when Avery opened her eyes. She'd fallen asleep earlier than anticipated. The sun was starting to rise, and Sprinkles was nowhere near awake yet. But when she stepped outside with her cup of coffee, the paper had already arrived.

There was only ever one reason why the paper would arrive earlier than usual. That was if there was some kind of breaking news. Avery glanced at her phone, certain that there would already be several messages from Deb about it.

She lifted the paper and recognized her own photographs splashed against the front page. She had almost forgotten that the mayor had leaked the photographs as a cover. But as she read, she couldn't help but smile.

She had expected the headline to refer to some kind of illicit affair. Instead, it read something entirely different. The police had gotten to the paper first.

MAYOR ARRESTED ON MURDER CHARGES,
LOVE TRIANGLE TURNS DEADLY.

The End.

Did you enjoy *Murder at the Festival*?

Then you should definitely check out
Murder at the Vineyard Inn!

A small town excited to celebrate their vet's wedding. A dead body found at the local inn. Innkeeper Avery Parker cannot afford to wait for the police to do their job.

Turn the page to start the first chapter!

Murder at the Vineyard Inn

SNEAK PEEK

Innkeeper and vineyard owner, Avery Parker, is thrilled to play a part in the town's long-awaited wedding.

Guests from near and far have gathered for what was meant to be a joyous union.

But instead of ringing toasts and happy cheers, a mysterious death casts a pall over the festivities.

When a dead body is discovered in her newly opened inn, Avery's dear friend is quickly put at the top of the suspect list.

Now it's up to Avery to prove her friend's innocence and discover the identity of the murderer before they strike again.

It's a race against time that could prove deadly if Avery fails. Will she be able to uncover the truth before it's too late?

Wine pairings and irresistible recipes included!

$\sim$

Chapter One

Eleanor and Samuel stood proudly at each other's side as they said their vows. The ceremony looked incredible.

In the small chapel were rows of benches decorated with the whitest lilies Avery had ever seen. Soft green accents and a softer dress code made it look truly magical. The light beamed through the chapel's stained-glass windows, painting an ethereal moment for all to enjoy.

Avery hardly recognized the town church as it was full of fresh flowers. She had also never seen Eleanor smile so brightly.

Everyone had pulled together to create a spectacular wedding. And it wasn't only the wedding that had occurred. Many festivities led up to their marriage, each one celebrating something else. There had been bridal showers and kitchen teas, and finally, the day of the ceremony had arrived, and all of them were relieved.

It seemed to Avery that the entire town had been invited. The church was packed full, and everyone watched as the couple pledged the remainder of their lives to each other. It took all her concentration for Avery not to cry.

It seemed not too long ago that Eleanor had told her how she simply wasn't interested in love anymore after her husband had died. And it wasn't long after that when she was introduced to the new town vet, Dr. Samuel Moses. Now, she stood gleaming, as she prepared to take his last name. It had been love at first sight, and the fact that they had made it to the point where they were married was no surprise to anyone.

Avery wondered if she would ever feel brave enough to look for love again. She'd lost her own husband in a boating accident, and it seemed like an impossible task to her. But it was clear to everyone present that Eleanor and Samuel loved each other deeply. So, Avery thought there might be hope for her to one day feel that kind of love again too.

A loud "AWWWW" traveled through the guests as Sprinkles carried the rings down the aisle. When Avery had first gotten him as a puppy, she wondered if he would ever learn to behave. And for the first few months, it seemed there wasn't much hope.

But after a couple of weeks of military-style dog training, Sprinkles had turned into the perfect golden retriever that she had hoped he would become. They had practiced walking that stretch down the aisle over and over again the days leading up to the wedding. So, naturally, Avery wanted to burst with pride when he did a perfect job of delivering the rings to the happy couple.

Avery waited at the back of the church, crouched low with a treat in her hand, for Sprinkles to return to her. She loved to see him with his white bow tie on and a proud puppy smile that he'd learned to give every time he'd successfully performed a new trick.

Sprinkles made his way back down the aisle toward Avery, soaking up the guests' praise as he passed them. And just as they had practiced, it seemed he would complete his task without any deviation.

That was until he got to the third row from the back. Sprinkles suddenly stopped and turned, pressing his nose against the hand of a man Avery didn't recognize. He was a tall man with thick dark hair. His suit looked as if it was just a little too tight, but purposely so.

He sported a very expensive watch, which he was careful to have on display. Everything about him seemed expensive. But what really bothered Avery was how he seemed to pay Sprinkles no attention at all. His hand rested carefully on his leg as he kept his eyes glued to the proceedings in front of him. There was something about him that seemed completely out of place. He sat upright and still as if he was poised for an audience.

Avery clicked her fingers as quietly as she could to get Sprinkles' attention. And to her surprise, it worked. Sprinkles looked at her and came walking casually down the rest of the aisle toward her, eager to receive his treat.

She looked back at the man, trying desperately to figure out who he was. But she could only see the back of his head. She did notice that he didn't seem to cheer and clap with the rest of the crowd. In fact, he didn't seem all that pleased to be there. The only movements he did make were to check that his watch was straight, his hair was neat, and his suit sat right. He reminded her of many of the businessmen she had seen during her time in the city.

The crowd cheered as the happy couple was finally pronounced Mr. and Mrs. Moses. The cameras flashed, and the crowd erupted once more as Samuel kissed his blushing bride. Soon, they were walking back toward the church doors as white rose petals rained down on them.

The ceremony had been perfect, just as Eleanor had hoped. Sprinkles sat patiently at the doors, accepting every loving pat and scruff the guests had to offer as they left the church. His white bow tie was sitting skew, but his smile remained fixed on his face.

By the time the reception was in full swing, Sprinkles was the life of the party. He spent most of his time waltzing between tables to see who would give him the most love and the most scraps of food from their plates.

Avery wondered if there was money to be made with Sprinkles working as a professional wedding guest for other weddings in town. He seemed to be a hit.

When Sprinkles nuzzled his snout into the hand of one of the guests, it reminded Avery of the man she had seen at the ceremony. So, she looked around the room to see if she could spot him. She knew the color of his suit and figured that perhaps if she saw him from the front, she might recognize him. There were many people in attendance who had scrubbed up well. Perhaps she did know the man and simply didn't recognize him in his finest clothes.

She scanned every table and every person on the dance floor and saw no sign of his tight navy blue suit. She knew that the speeches would soon commence, so she figured she'd find him when everybody stopped moving for a moment.

"What are you looking for?" Camille asked as she took a seat.

Camille was one of the women of the Stammtisch that Avery had joined. It was a group of women that often met on an informal basis, and Avery had come to care for the group quite a bit. It didn't surprise Avery that Camille, being the quietest of the lot, would be found nowhere near the dance floor.

"I'm looking for a man I saw earlier," Avery explained. "I didn't really recognize him from behind, so I figured I'd see if I recognized him from the front."

"That seems reasonable," Camille answered. "What did he look like from behind? Perhaps I can help you find him."

Avery was barely halfway through her description of him when Camille rolled her eyes. "That's Dean Scott," she said. "I saw him in the crowd as well, looking as sour as he usually does."

"You don't seem too pleased," Avery remarked. "I'm

assuming you're not a fan of his?"

"Nobody likes him," she explained. "I'm not surprised he left early. He wasn't even really invited."

"And what exactly makes him so unpopular?" Avery asked.

"Well, for one thing, he seems to think he's better than anyone here," Camille explained. "Especially since he moved to the city."

"Oh?"

"Yes, he keeps talking about how he has this big, fancy house there, but nobody's ever been invited to it," Camille answered. "And when he does come to town to visit his mother, he invites everyone over, and then we're basically forced to hear about how fantastic his life is."

"I see. So, he's a little boring?"

"Not boring, no. He's just one of those people whose ideas will always be better than yours. If you have something, his version of it is better...he likes to pretend that he's the most important person in the universe, and the rest of us were simply placed here to remind him of it."

"Sounds terrible," Avery said quietly.

"And he's not all that obvious about it, either," Camille continued. "You don't really notice how bad he makes you feel about yourself until he's left again. He does it all with a smile and a charm that can bamboozle anybody."

"Ah," Avery said. "That's called a narcissist."

"Well, that's precisely what he is," Camille laughed. "And if you ask him, he'd tell you that it's your fault for seeing him that way."

"I understand why he wasn't invited now," Avery laughed.

Camille stretched her eyes big. "And yet, he still came."

"He would, wouldn't he?" she asked. "You know, if he's a narcissist, it would probably drive him wild that everybody else was invited except him. He probably told himself it was just an admin error or something."

"That does sound like something he would do," Camille answered, taking a sip of her wine.

Le Blanc Cellars had gifted all the wine for the wedding, and Avery was starting to worry it wouldn't be enough. In every direction she looked, she saw another bottle being opened and more wine being poured. She wondered if she'd need to get a few more cases to last them the rest of the night. But then they'd finally reached the part of the night where the music slowed, and she knew most people had likely already had their fill.

"I heard he had his mother bring him as her plus one," Camille said.

"I'm sorry?" Avery asked. She'd been so worried about the wine she'd forgotten what they were talking about.

"Dean Scott," Camille said. "He was only able to come because his mother listed him as her date."

"His mother is Mrs. Scott!" Avery said, piecing it together. "She's the lady with the rose farm not too far from here."

"That's the one! And she's even worse than he is," Camille said.

"In what way?"

Avery didn't really know Mrs. Scott. She'd just caught glimpses of her here and there in town. She was an elderly woman with sleek gray hair. She only ever wore all-white clothes, and Avery was certain she'd never seen her without her red lipstick.

"She thinks she's more important than any of us," Camille said. "She once sold roses to some or other president, and in her mind that practically makes her royalty."

Avery laughed. "How did she find herself with an invitation then?"

"She's old!" Camille cried. "Eleanor felt too bad to tell her she couldn't come, especially since Mrs. Scott insisted on giving Eleanor half-price on her bouquet. So then, Eleanor had to invite her, and then that meant Dean found a way to get himself invited too."

"Do they have a habit of doing that?" Avery asked. "You know, worming their way into other people's affairs?"

"Oh yes, they're experts at it. You've been here long enough now. It's only a matter of time before Mrs. Scott starts poking her nose in your business too."

The way the man had looked and behaved made better sense to Avery now. Everything about him stood out to her, but she understood now that it had been his intention. He had wanted everyone to notice him.

She'd known too many people like that when she lived in the city. And she wondered if he had always been that way and was sculpted by his mother's attitude or if he had adopted that behavior in the city after he moved there.

She wondered what it was about him that had gotten Sprinkles' attention. There had to be something her dog found interesting about him, but she couldn't quite understand what. The more she thought through what Camille had told her, the more she understood the man.

His flashy watch made sense to her, and so did his tight suit. It also explained why he didn't join in the celebration with the rest of the guests. Narcissists are most unhappy when the attention is on someone else, especially if the other person is deserving of the attention they get.

Still, there was something about him that was familiar to her.

Get *Murder at the Vineyard Inn*
at your favorite retailer now!

Recipes

Eggs with Smoked Salmon and Mushrooms (serves 4)

4 large eggs
16 ounces cremini mushrooms
8 ounces smoked salmon
4 teaspoons butter
1 tablespoon water
salt
chopped green onion

- Clean mushrooms by wiping with dry paper towel.
- Slice mushrooms.
- Heat pan to medium and add 2 tsp butter.
- Add mushrooms and stir into butter.
- Salt and pepper to taste.
- Cook until brown and softened.
- Remove mushrooms from pan and set aside.
- Add remaining 2 tsp butter to pan.
- Crack eggs in hot pan, fry over medium heat.

- Add 1 tbsp water, cover pan.
- Once eggs are set, remove from heat.
- Divide mushrooms on four plates, top with 2 oz smoked salmon each.
- Carefully put egg over mixture and sprinkle with green onions.

Pairing options: Whipped Coffee or Strawberry Thyme Spritzer

Whipped Coffee (serves 4)

4 tablespoons instant coffee
4 tablespoons sugar
4 tablespoons boiling water
32 ounces milk

- In a small bowl, add coffee and sugar.
- Carefully pour in water.
- Whisk to combine (a hand mixer would be a better idea!).
- Coffee is ready once mixture is thick and a much lighter color (about 5-10 minutes).
- Divide milk equally between 4 glasses/mugs (this can be served over ice or hot).
- Divide frothy mixture between glasses or mugs.

Strawberry Thyme Spritzer (serves 4)

12 ounces vermouth, chilled
4 lemon wedges
8 strawberries thinly sliced
4 sprigs of thyme
crushed ice

8 ounces Prosecco

- Divide vermouth equally between 4 glasses.
- Squeeze juice of lemon wedge into each glass.
- Add strawberries and thyme equally between glasses.
- Add ice to each glass.
- Top with Prosecco.

Shrimp Étouffée (serves 6)

1 cup onion, diced
1 cup celery, diced
1 cup green bell pepper, diced
5 tablespoons butter
5 tablespoons flour
4 tablespoons tomato paste
1 pound of shrimp, shelled and deveined
4 cups of shrimp stock
1 cup green onions, sliced
1/2 cup flat leaf parsley, chopped
2 teaspoon salt
1/2 teaspoon black pepper
1 teaspoon cayenne pepper

- Heat pot to medium high, melt butter.
- Add onions, celery, and bell pepper to pot, stir.
- When softened, add flour and combine.
- Stir mixture for 10 minutes.
- Add tomato paste, cook another 10 minutes.
- Add shrimp to pot, cook for 5 minutes.
- Add stock. Cover and simmer for 5 minutes.
- Add green onions, parsley, salt, pepper, and cayenne pepper.
- Simmer 10 minutes.
- Remove pot from stove.
- Rest stew for 20 minutes.
- Plate stew over hot rice.

Shrimp Stock

- Boil shells and heads of shrimp with 6 cups of water for 15 minutes.

Pairing: Chenin Blanc or Chardonnay

Steak Florentine (serves 6)

2 large garlic cloves, cut in half
3 T-bone steaks (1½ pounds each, about 1½" -1 ¾"
thick)
Kosher salt and freshly ground black pepper
1 lemon, cut in half
2 teaspoons olive oil

- Rub garlic cloves all over steaks
- Sprinkle steaks with salt and pepper.
- Refrigerate 1 hour (overnight would be even better!).
- Let steaks come to room temperature (at least 20 minutes).
- Heat grill to medium-high.
- Grill steaks to preferred doneness. Only flip once and don't move after you've flipped them!
- Rare: 5 minutes per side
- Medium-rare: 7 minutes per side
- Rest steaks 10 minutes.
- Cut the meat away from the bone.
- Slice meat across the grain into 1" slices, squeeze lemon over, and drizzle sliced meat with olive oil.
- Serve with your favorite potatoes and grilled veggies.

Pairing: Sangiovese or Syrah

*Bee Sting Cake (serves 8)**
BATTER

4 large eggs
1 cup powdered sugar
½ cup all-purpose flour
1 tablespoon baking powder
½ teaspoon salt

FILLING

2 cups heavy cream
1 package instant vanilla pudding mix
2-3 tablespoons whole milk, if filling is too thick

TOPPING

1 cup sliced almonds
2 tablespoons sugar

GREASING PAN

½ teaspoon butter
1 teaspoon flour

- Preheat the oven to 350°F.
- Grease 9-inch springform pan with butter and sprinkle with flour.
- In a large bowl, beat eggs and powdered sugar with a mixer until creamy (5 minutes or so).
- Add flour, baking powder, and salt.
- Mix until well combined.
- Pour batter into pre-greased pan.
- Sprinkle batter with sugar and almonds.

- Bake cake at 350°F for 30 minutes (test with toothpick).
- Remove cake from pan and set aside to cool.
- In a medium bowl, beat pudding mix and heavy cream until thick, creamy, and spreadable (if mixture becomes too thick, add in 1-2 tablespoons of milk).
- Slice cooled cake horizontally in half, forming two layers.
- Spread filling evenly across the bottom layer.
- Place the top layer back.

Pairing: Hot black tea with a splash of milk

*This is kind of a cheater recipe, but I promise you it will taste just as lovely!

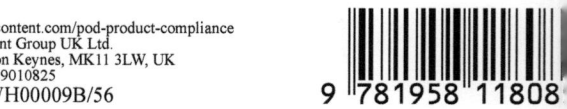